DON'T MISS THESE
ALL-ACTION WESTERN SERIES
FROM THE BERKLEY PUBLISHING GROUP

THE GUNSMITH by J. R. Roberts

Clint Adams was a legend among lawmen, outlaws, and ladies. They called him . . . the Gunsmith.

LONGARM by Tabor Evans

The popular long-running series about Deputy U.S. Marshal Custis Long—his life, his loves, his fight for justice.

SLOCUM by Jake Logan

Today's longest-running action Western. John Slocum rides a deadly trail of hot blood and cold steel.

BUSHWHACKERS by B. J. Lanagan

An action-packed series by the creators of Longarm! The rousing adventures of the most brutal gang of cutthroats ever assembled—Quantrill's Raiders.

DIAMONDBACK by Guy Brewer

Dex Yancey is Diamondback, a Southern gentleman turned con man when his brother cheats him out of the family fortune. Ladies love him. Gamblers hate him. But nobody pulls one over on Dex . . .

WILDGUN by Jack Hanson

The blazing adventures of mountain man Will Barlow—from the creators of Longarm!

TEXAS TRACKER by Tom Calhoun

J.T. Law: the most relentless—and dangerous—manhunter in all Texas. Where sheriffs and posses fail, he's the best man to bring in the most vicious outlaws—for a price.

THE GUNSMITH

351

THE TRIAL OF BAT MASTERSON

J. R. ROBERTS

JOVE BOOKS, NEW YORK

THE BERKLEY PUBLISHING GROUP
Published by the Penguin Group
Penguin Group (USA) Inc.
375 Hudson Street, New York, New York 10014, USA
Penguin Group (Canada), 90 Eglinton Avenue East, Suite 700, Toronto, Ontario M4P 2Y3, Canada
(a division of Pearson Penguin Canada Inc.)
Penguin Books Ltd., 80 Strand, London WC2R 0RL, England
Penguin Group Ireland, 25 St. Stephen's Green, Dublin 2, Ireland (a division of Penguin Books Ltd.)
Penguin Group (Australia), 250 Camberwell Road, Camberwell, Victoria 3124, Australia
(a division of Pearson Australia Group Pty. Ltd.)
Penguin Books India Pvt. Ltd., 11 Community Centre, Panchsheel Park, New Delhi—110 017, India
Penguin Group (NZ), 67 Apollo Drive, Rosedale, North Shore 0632, New Zealand
(a division of Pearson New Zealand Ltd.)
Penguin Books (South Africa) (Pty.) Ltd., 24 Sturdee Avenue, Rosebank, Johannesburg 2196,
South Africa

Penguin Books Ltd., Registered Offices: 80 Strand, London WC2R 0RL, England

This is a work of fiction. Names, characters, places, and incidents either are the product of the author's imagination or are used fictitiously, and any resemblance to actual persons, living or dead, business establishments, events, or locales is entirely coincidental.

THE TRIAL OF BAT MASTERSON

A Jove Book / published by arrangement with the author

PRINTING HISTORY
Jove edition / March 2011

Copyright © 2011 by Robert J. Randisi.
Cover illustration by Sergio Giovine.

ISBN: 978-0-515-14907-4

JOVE®
Jove Books are published by The Berkley Publishing Group,
a division of Penguin Group (USA) Inc.,
375 Hudson Street, New York, New York 10014.
JOVE® is a registered trademark of Penguin Group (USA) Inc.
The "J" design is a trademark of Penguin Group (USA) Inc.

PRINTED IN THE UNITED STATES OF AMERICA

10 9 8 7 6 5 4 3 2 1

ONE

Bat Masterson stared at the cards in his hands. It was his best hand of the night, coming at a good time, when the game was drawing to a close.

He was in Sweetwater, Colorado, had been there for three days, and playing in this game for the past two nights. The game would start at about midnight, continue on after closing, finish up by first light.

He could tell by looking at the window that dawn was approaching. He looked across the table at Cable Lockheart. So far, Cable had owned him. This hand was Bat's last chance to save face, maybe break even or—if he played the cards right—get ahead.

The dealer, Ralph Ward, said to Tom Nolan, "To you, Tom."

"I open for twenty," Nolan said.

"Bat?"

Bat took a chance and said, "I call."

Ben Craddock called, and then Cable raised.

"Up fifty," he said.

Back to the dealer, who called. Nolan called. Bat wanted to raise, but he said, "I call."

Craddock looked at the window. "Looks like the last hand. I might as well call."

Cable looked across the table at Bat and grinned. "Last chance, Bat," he said.

Bat simply shrugged.

"Cards?" Ward asked.

"Three," Nolan said.

"I'll take one," Bat said.

"Three," Craddock said.

"I'll take two," Cable said.

"Dealer takes three," Ward said.

"Nolan, you opened," Ward said.

"I check to the raiser."

"Bat?"

Bat could have checked to trap Cable, but betting would send a message that he had something. The size of the bet would dictate how good a hand he had. He didn't want to seem too strong so he said, "I bet forty."

"I fold," Craddock said.

The bet was to Cable. He stared across the table at Bat, grinning. "Forty, huh? And you drew one card? Made your straight? A flush?"

Bat just shrugged.

"Okay, then," Cable said. "I raise a hundred."

"I fold," Ward said.

"Me, too," Tom Nolan said.

"You and me, Bat," Cable said. "Whaddaya gonna do?"

Without hesitating, Bat said, "Your hundred, and another two hundred."

Cable laughed. He was young, arrogant, and prime to be taken.

"Tryin' ta get it all back in one hand?" he asked. "I'll oblige you." He pushed his money into the pot. "A thousand dollars, give or take."

Craddock whistled.

"Count it?" Ward asked.

"Never mind," Bat said. "You're covered, Cable."

"Am I?" the man asked. "I don't see the money in the pot."

"Bat's good for it," Ward said.

"It's okay, Ralph." Bat reached into his jacket, where he had a thousand-dollar bill pinned to the lining. He took it out, set it down on the table, smoothed it, and pushed it into the pot.

"You're covered," he said. "I should raise you because you're an arrogant ass, but then we'd have to wait for you to come up with the money."

Cable bristled at that. "Go ahead and raise," he growled. "I'm good for it!"

"No," Ward said, "you ain't."

Cable gave Ward a murderous look.

"Never mind," Bat said. "I covered your bet, Cable. Whaddaya got?"

Cable laid his hand down triumphantly. "Kept the three jacks I was dealt, and drew two fives to it," he said. "A full house!"

He started to reach for the money on the table.

"No good," Bat said.

"What?" Cable asked.

Bat laid down his hand. "Four eights."

"You drew one card," Cable said. "You had a pat hand and you drew a card?"

"Why not?" Bat asked.

The other players at the table started to laugh, which

Cable couldn't take. He stood up so quickly his chair went over backwards.

"Don't draw, Cable," Ward said. "Bat'll kill you."

Cable stood there, shaking with rage and humiliation.

"He outplayed you, boy," Nolan said. "Take it like a man and walk away."

Cable glared at all four men, then one last time at Bat before turning and storming out of the saloon.

"You got him good on that one, Bat," Ward said.

"Better watch that boy," Ben Craddock said. "He's got backshooter written all over him."

"I'll watch it," Bat said. He pocketed his winnings and returned his emergency thousand to the lining of his jacket.

"Same time tomorrow, gents?" Ward asked.

"Not sure I'll be here tomorrow," Bat said. "We'll just have to wait and see."

Craddock said, "Well, I've got to get some sleep."

"My wife will have breakfast waitin' for me," Ward said.

"That's a good woman you've got there, Ralph," Bat said, "Better keep her."

"I intend to."

All four men stepped outside the saloon, pulling the door closed behind them. Craddock went to get his sleep, Ward his breakfast.

"Where you headed, Bat?" Tom Nolan asked.

"My hotel."

"Feel like some breakfast?"

"I think I'll catch some sleep, get some lunch, and then decide what to do next, Tom," Bat said. "See you."

"Take care," Nolan said.

He watched as Bat walked toward his hotel, then turned and walked the other way.

The next time he saw Bat Masterson, the man was behind bars.

TWO

The telegram found Clint Adams in Labyrinth, Texas. The request was succinct: "Come to Sweetwater, Colorado right away. Bat Masterson in trouble." It was signed "Tom Nolan."

Clint didn't know a Tom Nolan, but he certainly knew Bat Masterson, and knowing that Bat was in trouble was all the reason he needed to ride for Sweetwater at top speed.

As he rode down the main street of Sweetwater steam rose from the withers of Eclipse, his Darley Arabian.

"Sorry for the push, big fella," he said, patting the horse's neck, "but you'll get some rest now."

He rode to the livery stable, where the liveryman gave him a hard look. "Shouldn't be pushing a horse like this that hard," he scolded Clint.

"I know it," Clint said, "but it was an emergency. Take good care of him."

"I will," the man said, his tine indicating that Clint obviously didn't—but Clint couldn't worry about that now.

He left the livery with his saddlebags and rifle and stopped at the first hotel he came to, with the unfortunate name of the Cherry Blossom Hotel. Sweetwater was a decent-sized town, with enough side streets to house many hotels and saloons. But Clint didn't need luxury. He just needed a room with a bed.

"Sir?" the young desk clerk asked. "Can I help you?"

"I'm looking for a man named Tom Nolan. Do you know him?"

"Well, yes, sir, Mr. Nolan is—"

"I don't care what he is," Clint said. "Can you get a message to him for me?"

"I suppose so."

"Good," Clint said. "Give me a room and then get a message to him that Clint Adams is here."

"C-Clint Adams?"

"That's right."

"Umm, okay."

The clerk stared at him.

"A room?" Clint asked.

"Oh, yeah," the young man said. He grabbed a key from behind him. "Room four."

Clint grabbed the key.

"Get that message to him, right away."

"Yessir."

As Clint headed for the stairs the clerk said, "Mr. Adams?"

"Yeah?"

"Is this about the Bat Masterson thing?"

Clint stopped with one foot on the first step. "What Bat Masterson thing?"

"Uh, the murder."

Clint turned, walked back to the desk with a cold feeling in the pit of his stomach.

"What murder?" Clint asked. "Bat Masterson was murdered?"

"Oh, no," the clerk said. "He's in jail, charged with murder."

Clint felt relieved. This must have been the reason the telegram was sent.

"Get that message to Tom Nolan," Clint said. "Tell him I want to see him as soon as possible."

"Yessir," the clerk said. "I'll take care of it right away."

Clint poked the clerk in the chest with his forefinger and said, "Do it sooner."

"Y-yessir!"

Clint went up to the second floor, found room four, and let himself in. He looked out the window, saw the clerk hurrying across the street.

Expecting Tom Nolan—whoever he was—to come right over, Clint removed his shirt, used the pitcher and basin to wash the trail dust from his face and chest, then donned a clean shirt and settled down to wait.

A knock came at the door in fifteen minutes. He answered with his gun in hand.

"Clint Adams?" the man in the hall asked.

"That's right."

"I'm Tom Nolan," the man said. He was in his forties, neatly dressed, and not wearing a gun. "I sent you the telegram, You made good time."

"I pushed," Clint said, "hoping I wouldn't be too late."

"Bat's been in a cell for a week," Nolan said. "We're still waitin' for the circuit judge to get here."

"Who's the lawman who arrested him?"

"His name's Deming," Nolan said, "Sheriff Al Deming. Been the law here in Sweetwater for years."

"If Bat's being railroaded, would the sheriff be in on it?"

"Normally, I'd say no, but I guess anything's possible."

"Why'd you send me a telegram?"

"I figured Bat needed all the help he could get," Nolan said. "He's talked about you the way a man talks about a good friend."

"Did he ask you to send for me?"

"No," Nolan said, "it was my idea."

"Well, it was a good one," Clint said, finally holstering his gun. "Can you take me to him?"

"Right now, if you want," Nolan said.

"I want."

During the walk from the hotel to the jail, Clint asked, "Who's he supposed to have killed?"

"A kid named Cable Lockheart," Nolan said, "fancies himself a gambler. Bat made a fool of him at the table after Cable had been beating him for two days."

"That sounds like Bat," Clint said, "but it also sounds like a motive for this Lockheart to have killed Bat, not the other way around."

"I know," Nolan said, "that's what Bat said, but he was found in the room with Cable's body, standing over him."

"Doesn't sound like Bat to get himself in trouble that way," Clint said. "Why would he do that? Stand there and let himself be found that way?"

"That's somethin' you're gonna have to ask him," Tom Nolan said.

THREE

Clint followed Tom Nolan to the sheriff's office and inside. The lawman and one of his deputies were there. They turned as the door opened and the two men entered.

"Nolan," the Sheriff said.

"Sheriff Deming," Nolan said, "this is Clint Adams."

"The Gunsmith?" the young deputy asked, staring in awe.

"That's right," Nolan said.

"What's the Gunsmith want in Sweetwater?" Deming asked.

"I want to talk to Bat Masterson," Clint said.

"Why's that?"

"He's a friend of mine."

If Deming wondered how Clint knew that Bat Masterson was in his jail, he didn't ask.

"I'll need your gun," Deming said.

"Of course." Clint took his gun from his holster and

handed it to the lawman. It was a very unnatural act for him, and felt that way.

"Come on," Deming said, "I'll take you back."

Clint followed the sheriff's broad back to the cellblock. The sheriff grabbed the keys from a peg on the wall, opened the thick wooden door.

"Just knock when you're finished," he said, "and I'll let you out."

Clint entered the cellblock and the sheriff closed and locked the door behind him.

Inside were three cells, and only the middle one was occupied. Bat Masterson was lying on his back, his forearm thrown across his eyes. His jacket was stuffed between a set of bars, his once-white shirt dark with grime.

"What the hell have you gotten yourself into this time?" Clint asked.

"That who I think it is?" Bat asked, without removing his arm from his eyes.

"It is," Clint said. "I've come to get you out."

"Gonna break me out?"

"I was kind of thinking about trying to prove you innocent first."

Now Bat dropped his arm, sat up, and swung his feet to the floor.

"Leave it to you to think of that first," he said. He stood up, approached the bars, and clasped hands with his friend.

"How'd you get here?" he asked.

"Nolan sent me a telegram," Clint said. "He a friend of yours?"

"A new friend," Bat admitted, then added, "maybe one of my best friends, now. Just get in?"

"I came over as soon as I heard," Clint said. "Is it true you were found standing over the dead man?"

"Well," Bat said, "he was in my room. I was kind of confused at the time, and then the door slammed open and the sheriff stood there."

"Tipped off."

"Obviously."

"So you were set up."

"Again, obviously."

"Okay," Clint said, "let's start with who would want to frame you?"

"Beats me," Bat said. "The only person in town who disliked me that much was the dead man."

"That's not very helpful, Bat," Clint said. "What happened?"

"The dead man, Lockheart, had been beating me for two days. I don't know how. I had the worst run of luck—until the last hand, when I got dealt four of a kind. I slow played it, drew one card, and then . . . bam! I dropped the hammer. Got all my money back."

"How much we talking about?"

"Not a lot," Bat said. "It wasn't a very high-stakes game. It was more the humiliation, I think, for Lockheart. He was sure his full house was gonna clean me out."

"So?"

"Well, for a minute I thought I was going to have to kill him right then and there, but then he turned and stormed out. I went to my room, and there he was, shot to death on my floor."

"How much time went by since the time he left and the time you got to your room?"

"Maybe twenty minutes," Bat said.

"And in that time somebody managed to get him to your room, and kill him?"

"Looks like. Or else he was waiting for me in my room, and somebody got him."

"Maybe to help you out? Only you got blamed."

Bat shrugged.

"Bat, that's giving with one hand and taking with the other, isn't it?"

"I suppose."

"And that's your whole story?"

"That's it."

"You got a lawyer?"

"Sort of."

"What's that mean?"

"There are a few in town, but the only one who'd touch me is a kid. His name's Lee Martin."

Clint had worked with young lawyers in the past, notably in Hannibal, Missouri. They were very eager, and not always as talented.

"I'll talk to him," Clint said. "Maybe I can be a character witness."

"I'd really rather this never went to trial," Bat said. "After all, I am the stranger in town."

"Yeah, but the famous one."

"All the more reason they might want to put me away," Bat said.

"What do you mean?"

"Might put this town on the map," Bat said, "the town that convicted Bat Masterson of murder."

FOUR

Clint knocked on the cellblock door and the sheriff opened it.

"Finished?"

"For now."

Deming closed the door and locked it. Nolan was still there. The deputy had gone. Deming gave Clint back his gun. He holstered it.

"You learn anything?" Deming asked.

"Only what I already knew."

"And what's that?"

"That Bat didn't do it."

"So he says."

"Where's his gun?"

The sheriff opened the bottom drawer of his desk, took out a gun and holster, and set it atop the desk. Clint picked it up and sniffed it.

"Hasn't been fired lately, or cleaned," he said.

"He didn't use his own gun," Deming said. "He shot Cable with Cable's own gun."

"Cable?"

"Cable Lockheart, the dead man."

"Who was he?"

"Just a local kid who thought he was a gambler," Deming said. "I guess Masterson proved him wrong."

"Lockheart popular in town?"

"No," Deming said, "nobody really liked him."

"So anybody could have killed him, then?"

"No," the sheriff said, "only a stranger in town would be that dumb."

"Don't tell me, let me guess," Clint said. "His father's a rich rancher."

"No, his father was a drunk."

"So his mother does everybody's laundry? Everybody loves her?"

"His mother was a whore," Deming said. "Both his parents are dead."

"So what's everybody afraid of?"

"Not what," Deming said. "Who."

"And who would that be?"

"His brother."

"Who's his brother?" Clint asked, wondering how many more questions he was going to have to ask to get the man to the point.

"You heard of Mason Locke?"

"Locke?" Clint asked. "For Lockheart?"

"That's right."

"His brother is a gunfighter?"

"His brother," Deming said, "is one of the fastest guns alive. Maybe even faster than you."

"Have you heard of Mason Locke?" Tom Nolan asked.

"Hasn't everyone?"

"I haven't."

"How long have you lived here?" Clint asked.

"I don't live here," Nolan said.

Clint stopped him, putting his hand on his arm. "I thought you were a local?"

"No," Nolan said, "I got here about a week before Bat did."

"So why are you still here?"

"I wouldn't run out on Bat," Nolan said. "After I sent you the telegram and you answered, saying you were comin', I figured I'd stay."

They started walking again.

"So who's Mason Locke?"

"He's a killer," Clint said, "and he's not going to like it when he hears his brother's dead."

"You think he'll come here?"

"Oh, he'll come."

"For Bat?"

"Why else?"

"Do you think the sheriff will give Bat to him?" Nolan asked.

"I'm here to make sure that doesn't happen."

"B-but the sheriff said that this fella Locke is faster than you. Is that true?"

"I don't know," Clint said.

"Is he faster than Bat?"

"I don't know that either, Tom," Clint said. "I guess we're going to have to wait and see."

"Hey," Nolan said, "why don't we break Bat out?"

Clint looked at Nolan. In that moment, he realized the man was younger than he'd thought. Not late thirties, but early thirties.

"We're not going to break him out, Tom," Clint said. "That would be against the law."

"The law that has Bat behind bars for somethin' he didn't do?"

"How do you know he didn't do it?"

"He told me."

"And that's enough for you?"

"Well, yeah . . . ain't it enough for you?"

"Yes, it is," Clint said, "but I've known Bat for a long time, and you only just met him."

"That may be true," Nolan said, "but he's Bat Masterson!"

"Yeah," Clint said, "he is."

FIVE

Clint and Nolan went to the nearest saloon and, over beers, Clint had Nolan tell him about the other players in the poker game.

"Craddock, he run the feed and grain store," Nolan said. "Ralph Ward is the owner of the mercantile, and the hardware store."

"So Bat's been playing low-stakes poker with a couple of town fathers, the brother of a gunfighter, and . . ."

"And me," Nolan said.

"You?"

"And it wasn't low stakes," Nolan said. "That last pot, Bat took a thousand-dollar-bill from inside his jacket and tossed it into the pot."

"His emergency thousand?"

Nolan nodded.

"Was that the biggest pot of the night?"

Nolan nodded again.

"And it was down to Lockheart and Bat?"

"Too rich for the rest of us."

"Did you think Lockheart was going to go for his gun?" Clint asked.

"Sure looked like it, but he got smart and walked out."

"And, apparently, went to Bat's room to wait for him," Clint said. "At least, that's what the sheriff thinks."

"And then Bat killed him with Cable's own gun?" Nolan asked. "If Cable was waitin' for him, why wouldn't Bat just kill him as soon as he walked in? Using his gun?"

"That's not what the sheriff's thinking," Clint said. "He seems to have his mind made up. There's one thing I'm not sure of."

"What's that?"

"Whether we're waiting for the circuit judge," Clint said, "or Mason Locke."

It was still early so Clint decided to go and talk to the other poker players.

He found Ben Craddock in his store, where the man took the time to talk to him about that night.

"Seemed to me Lockheart was just lookin' to get himself killed," he said.

"And do you think Bat obliged him?"

Craddock hesitated. "I don't know Masterson well, Mr. Adams," Craddock said. "Before I played poker with him, all I knew was his reputation."

"And after playing poker with him?"

Craddock rubbed his lantern jaw. "I guess if Bat was gonna kill him, he'd'a done it right there at the table," Craddock said. "Cable was askin' for it. Sure looked like he was gonna go for his gun."

"Bat let him walk."

Craddock nodded.

"Okay, Mr. Craddock," Clint said. "Thanks for sharing your thoughts."

"You gonna try to prove Bat didn't do it?"

"I am."

"Seems to me you'd have to find out who did."

"That's the way it seems to me, too."

"You know, the people in this town would stand aside when Cable walked down the street, only they weren't standin' aside for him."

"I know about his brother, Mr. Craddock."

"When he hears, he's gonna come to town."

"Do you know Mason Locke?"

"Knew him when he lived in town," Craddock said. "Ain't seen him for ten years."

"You know what kind of man he is?"

"I know what kind of man he was, but that was ten years ago," Craddock said. "Don't seem that'd be important now."

"No," Clint said, "I guess not. Thanks again."

Nolan was waiting outside to guide Clint to Ralph Ward. They checked the mercantile first, didn't find him there, then went to the hardware store.

As they entered, Nolan said, "That's him behind the counter."

"Okay," Clint said, "you can wait outside, Tom."

"Okay."

Nolan left and Clint approached the counter. There were no customers, and Ward looked up immediately.

"Help you, sir?" he asked from underneath a well-cared-for handlebar mustache.

"My name's Clint Adams, Mr. Ward," Clint said. "I'm a friend of Bat Masterson's."

"Too bad about Masterson," Ward said. "Sure enjoyed playin' poker with him."

"Are you thinking Bat actually did kill Cable Lockheart?"

"Well," Ward said, looking confused, "that's what people have been sayin'."

"That's what the sheriff says, too," Clint commented.

"You don't believe he done it?"

"I don't, and I'm going to prove it."

"How you plannin' to do that?"

"By finding out who really did."

"Well, I wish you luck. I don't know anybody in this town fool enough to make a move against Cable, not when you know who his brother is."

"Well, maybe somebody decided to do it and blame Bat," Clint said. "You got any idea who would want Cable dead?"

"Lotsa folks, I imagine," Ward said. "Cable wasn't a likeable guy."

"But nobody specific?"

"Can't think of anybody."

"Well, I'm over at the Cherry Blossom," Clint said. "If anything occurs to you, please let me know."

"I will," Ward said.

Clint shook hands with the man and went outside, where Nolan was still waiting.

SIX

It took four days for the news of his brother's death to reach Mason Locke.

He was wearing out a whore in Flint, Michigan, when there was a knock on the hotel room door.

"Go away," he bellowed without slowing down. He had the blonde on her back, heavy thighs spread wide, and was plowing the hell out of her. She was a big girl, which was just how he liked them. With every thrust he grunted, and she cried out because she knew he liked it when she was loud.

"Oooh, yeah," she said, urging him on, "come on, Mason . . ."

Her name was Christy, and she knew how to put on a good show so that the man with her felt special. Whenever Locke was in town and wanted a whore, he asked for Christy. It didn't much matter to him if she was faking or not. He knew he wasn't faking, and that was all that mattered to him.

The knock came again.

"Goddamnit! I'm busy!"

"Got some news for you, Mason."

It was his partner, Red Cassiday.

"You're gonna wanna hear it."

Reluctantly, Locke withdrew his hard dick from Christy's sopping pussy and walked to the door, naked. Very comfortable with her own nudity, the whore did nothing to cover herself up.

Mason Locke slammed the door open and said, "What the hell is it?"

Red looked at him sadly and said, "I, uh, just heard that, uh, Cable got hisself killed."

Locke hesitated a moment. Red looked past him to the naked woman, her big floppy tits and wide-open fat thighs, so he wouldn't have to look at his naked partner.

"Where?"

"Sweetwater."

"When?"

"'Bout four days ago."

"Who killed him?"

"They're sayin' he was shot by Bat Masterson."

Locke stopped to think again. "Okay," he said, "wait for me downstairs."

"You comin' right down?"

"When I'm done here!" Locke snapped, and slammed the door.

"What's wrong, lover?" Christy asked when he came back to bed.

"Nothin'. My stupid brother finally got hisself killed."

"Oh, I'm sorry," she said. She started to get off the bed.

"Where the hell are you goin'?" he demanded, blocking her way.

"I thought you'd wanna—"

He grabbed her, hauled her back onto the bed, pushed her down on her back, and grabbed her ankles.

"Does this look like I'm done?" he asked, showing her his raging erection.

"Uh, well no, but your brother—"

"He'll still be dead when we're finished here," he said. "I'm gonna fuck you 'til your ears bleed, girlie."

Christy grinned at him and said, "Let me have it, Daddy."

He spread her ankles, pressed the head of his penis to her wet vagina and pushed. He slid right into her to the hilt, causing her to catch her breath.

"Damn!" she said.

He started to fuck her, in and out, faster and faster, trying to keep himself from thinking about Cable for the time being. Might as well finish what he was doing, because after this poke was done all he was going to be interested in was avenging his brother's death.

He may have been a stupid ass, but he was still his brother.

As Locke came out, he saw Red Cassiday waiting on the front steps. He had saddled the horses and tied them to a post.

"Ready to go?" Red asked.

"I'm ready," Locke said.

As he and Red started for the horses, three men appeared from the other side of the building.

"The Hopper Gang," Red said.

"They've been lookin' for us," Locke said. "Looks like they found us."

"What do we do?"

"This ain't the time to fool around," Locke said, "so we take 'em."

SEVEN

"Andy's the faster gun," Locke said. "He's in the middle. I'll take him, and Frank to his right. You take Joe."

"Thought you could steal from us and get away?" Andy Hopper called out.

"I was hopin', Andy," Locke said. "That way we wouldn't have to kill you."

Andy stopped walking, his brothers followed his lead. They fanned out a bit, making some space between the three.

"Too bad, Mason," Andy Hopper said.

"We'd return the money we took," Locke said, "but we spent it."

"Wouldn't matter," Andy said. "Even if you gave it back, we'd still kill you."

"You mean, you'd try," Locke said.

"Three to two, Mason," Andy said, "and I think I can take you. So my brothers will take care of Red. I like the odds."

"I have a better idea, Andy," Locke said. "Turn around and leave."

Instead of answering, Andy Hopper went for his gun. He was fast, but he was also wrong. He was no match for Mason Locke.

Locke drew, killed Andy, then shot Frank before the man could touch his gun. Red Cassiday had still not fired, so Locke turned his attention to Joe Hopper and shot him through the heart.

He ejected his spent shells, replaced them, and holstered his gun.

"Jesus," Red said.

Locke looked at his partner.

"I never got off a shot," Red said.

"Well," Locke said, "I guess you'll have to get some practice in."

They walked to their horses, wanting to ride out before the law showed up.

"I know you're fast," Red said, as they rode out. "I'm just always shocked by how fast."

Sometimes, Locke thought, it surprised him, too.

That was several days ago, and now he and Red were on the trail, heading for Sweetwater. Locke was not having them push their horses. He was in no hurry.

"Whaddaya gonna do when we get there, Mace?" Red asked.

"Whaddaya think?" Locke asked. "I'm gonna kill Bat Masterson."

"But . . . he'll be in jail."

"Then we'll haul his ass out of jail."

"But . . . he's Bat Masterson."

"I don't care if he's Jesus Christ himself," Mason Locke said. "A bullet will kill him."

"And then what?"

"And then we'll take care of that town."

"Why?" Red asked. "What did the town do?"

"They let him die," Locke said. "They stood by and let him die."

"So what're we gonna do?"

Locke turned his head and looked at his partner riding beside him. "We're gonna burn it to the ground, Red," he said. "We're gonna burn that town to the ground."

"The whole town?"

"The whole goddamned town," Locke said.

EIGHT

"Mason Locke?" Bat asked. "I've heard of him."

Clint was sitting outside the cell, Bat inside. There was a wooden crate in front of the cell, with cards on it.

First Clint had eaten with Bat, both their meals coming from a nearby café, and now they were playing poker two-handed. Clint chose that moment to tell Bat about Cable Lockheart's brother.

"Nobody mentioned that to you?" Clint asked.

"No," Bat said, shuffling the cards. "I guess nobody wanted to scare me."

"I'd be scared if Mason Locke came here and I was in a cell without a gun."

"No, you wouldn't," Bat said.

"Why not?"

"Because if you were in the cell, you'd have me outside, just like I have you." He dealt out five cards.

They played poker for about two hours before the sheriff came in.

"Time to shut it down, gents," he said.

"Bedtime?" Bat asked.

"That's right."

"This early?" Clint asked.

"I make the rules here, Adams," Deming said.

"Hey," Clint said, putting up his hands, "not trying to change the rules." He stood up and left the cards and crate where they were. "I'll see you in the morning, Bat," he said.

"Sure thing, Clint," Bat said. "I'll be here."

Clint went out the door to the office. Sheriff Deming waited until he heard Clint go out the front door, then he turned and kicked the crate. Cards flew everywhere.

"'Night, Masterson," he said. He blew out the lamp in the wall and went into the office.

Bat had no choice but to recline on his cot. It was good to have Clint in Sweetwater working on his behalf, but with Mason Locke on the way he was starting to think about breaking out. Not to try to escape, just to be able to defend himself. He knew Clint would defend him with his own life, and he trusted his friend. He was just used to defending himself.

He wondered if he could get Clint to agree to break him out.

Clint left the sheriff's office and went across the street to the Little Nugget Saloon. It was the saloon where the infamous poker game had taken place, and Clint thought it was about time he checked over the establishment.

He went inside. The place was busy, but he found space at the bar and ordered a beer, then turned and looked the place over. There were a couple of poker games going on, but neither of them had Ralph Ward or Ben Craddock.

"Hey handsome," one of the saloon girls said, sidling up alongside him. "I'm Jenny. Want some company?"

She was brunette, about twenty-five, very pretty but also very thin. She was wearing a gown and where most girls would have showed some bosom she featured a flat chest.

"Not right now, thanks, Jenny," he said.

"Well, just let me know if you change your mind."

As she walked off the batwing doors opened and Tom Nolan came in. He spotted Clint and walked right over.

"How's Bat?"

"As well as can be expected," Clint said. "I ate with him, and played some poker."

Nolan waved at the bartender and then accepted a beer.

"Well, this is the place," he said to Clint.

"So I see," Clint said. "Tell me, did Cable have any friends at all?"

"I haven't been here in town long enough to answer that question," Nolan said.

"So you know who we can ask?"

"Well . . . I understand there's a woman."

"A woman? A wife?"

"Not a wife," Nolan said. "I guess a girlfriend."

"What's her name?"

"I think he mentioned her name was Angie."

"Angie what?"

Nolan shrugged.

"Okay," Clint said, "tomorrow we'll try and find her. Maybe she can tell us who would have wanted to kill Cable Lockheart."

"So what do we do in the meantime?"

"I'm going to finish this beer and then go to my room and read."

"Sure you wouldn't rather play some poker?" Nolan asked. "There are two seats open."

"The game will go on?"

"As far as I know," Nolan said, "Ward and Craddock play every night. It's only the other players who change, from time to time."

"And when does the game start?"

"Midnight."

"Where?"

Nolan pointed.

"That empty table. Nobody else is allowed to sit there."

"And will both players be replaced?"

"If you agree to play, they will."

Clint thought it over. Maybe it might do some good to watch Ward and Craddock play. Maybe one of them would remember or say something helpful during the game.

"You know what?" Clint asked. "I think I will play."

"Good," Nolan said, "be here at midnight."

Clint nodded, started to leave, then turned back.

"Tell me something: How did you get in to the game?" he asked.

"I came in one night. One seat was empty. I sat in it. There ya go."

"Okay," Clint said. "I'll come in later. If there's an empty seat, I'll take it."

NINE

Clint reentered the Little Nugget at about eleven forty-five. Still open, still pretty busy, Tom Nolan still at the bar. Other poker games still going on. Girls still working the floor.

At the previously empty table now sat both Ward and Craddock.

"They look eager," Clint said, coming up next to Nolan.

"Without Bat in the game, one of them might actually win."

"You and me makes four," Clint said. "Who's the fifth player?"

Nolan shrugged. "Might not even be one. We'll have to wait and see. You want a beer?"

"I don't drink while I'm playing poker," Clint told him. "Think they'll mind if I sit in?"

"Table rule," Nolan said. "Empty seat, anybody can sit in."

"Interesting rule."

"Wanna get started?" Nolan asked.

"You go ahead," Clint said. "I'll be along in a minute."

"Suit yourself."

Nolan carried his beer over to the table and sat down.

With three players at the table, Ralph Ward started dealing.

Clint watched them for twenty minutes. When nobody else sat in, he walked over.

"Evening, gents," Clint said. "I understand anybody can sit in?"

Ward looked up and said, "Adams?"

Craddock said, "Sit down. Table rule says anybody can sit in."

Clint took a seat from which he could view the entire floor.

"Anybody else coming?" he asked, looking pointedly at the empty chair.

"Could be," Ward said. "Dealer's choice, money plays. No chips."

"Suits me," Clint said, taking his money out.

"Craddock deals," Ward said.

Craddock picked up the cards, shuffled, allowed Ward to cut the deck, then dealt out five cards, facedown.

"Draw poker," he said.

After a few hours, the saloon started to empty out, and so did the pokes of the other three players. Clint was winning three out of every four hands, and while the stakes were not high, his profits were mounting.

"How long does this game go on?" he asked.

"'Til first light," Ward said.

"Whose idea was that?"

"Neither Ralph or me can sleep," Craddock said, "so we came up with this game a few years ago. We start, anybody else who wants to play can sit in."

"Is it ever just the two of you?"

"It has been, on occasion," Ward said, "but usually some interested party sits in."

"And the saloon owner lets you stay here all night?" Clint asked.

"He does," Craddock said, "and he trusts us with his keys so we can lock up when we leave. You gonna play cards, Adams?"

"Sure, sorry," Clint said. He looked at his cards. "I open for ten."

By daybreak, a fifth player had not arrived, and the game broke up.

"You fellas do this every night?" Clint asked with a yawn as they all headed for the door.

"Every night," Ward said.

"And what do you do now?"

"Now we go home to sleep," Craddock said.

"Or breakfast and then sleep," Ward said.

They went outside and Ward closed and locked the front door.

"See you gents tonight," he said, walking away.

"'Night, boys," Craddock said, walking the other way.

Clint watched them both go, then looked at Nolan.

"Didn't learn very much from that, did you?" Nolan asked.

"No," Clint said, "but I did make myself a few extra dollars."

"How about tonight?"

"That depends."

"On what?"

"On whether or not we find Cable Lockheart's girl-friend, Angie ."

TEN

In the morning, Clint left his hotel and found a place to have breakfast. It wasn't good, but it was off the main street, and the coffee was drinkable.

He'd forgotten one important thing he had to do. He should have done it the day before, but now he'd have to do it today. Nolan wanted to help, so maybe he'd charge the man with finding Angie. He had to go and see Bat's young lawyer, Lee Martin.

He finished his breakfast, walked out, and headed for the sheriff's office.

"You want to see your friend again?" the sheriff asked as he walked in.

"Not right now," Clint said. "That is, if you can tell me where to find Lee Martin."

"The kid lawyer? He's got an office on Second Street, above a ladies' hat shop." Deming laughed. "Ya can't miss it."

"Thanks, Sheriff."

"Oh," Deming said, as Clint was leaving, "you might be interested to know the circuit judge will be here in three days."

Clint stopped and turned to look back at the sheriff.

"Three days?" Clint asked. "That probably gives Mason Locke time to beat him here, doesn't it?"

Deming stood up.

"What are you tryin' to say?"

"That maybe you figure if Locke gets here first he'll save everybody the trouble of a trial."

"I gotta admit," Deming said, "it don't matter to me who gets here first, but it ain't like I'm plannin' anything."

"I hope not," Clint said, "for your sake."

"Are you threatenin' me?" Deming asked. "Threatenin' the law?"

"I don't make threats, Sheriff," Clint said, "especially not to a lawman. I'm just telling you how it is."

Deming tried to stare Clint down, but in the end he averted his eyes and Clint walked out.

Clint went back to his hotel, where he found Tom Nolan waiting in the lobby.

"I thought you were still upstairs," Nolan said.

"I went out early and had breakfast."

"I thought we were gonna have breakfast together."

"Did we say that? Sorry. I was hungry. And I had something to do."

"Well . . . what do we do now?"

"I need to go and talk to the lawyer who's working for Bat," Clint said. "What I need you to do is find the girl, Angie. I'll need to talk to her after I'm finished with the lawyer."

"Okay," Nolan said. "When I find her, where should I take her?"

Clint thought a moment, then said, "Just bring her here. Wait with her in the lobby and I'll be back."

"What if I can't find her?"

"Why should she be hard to find unless she's hiding?" Clint asked. And why would she hide?"

"Maybe she thinks whoever killed Cable wants to kill her."

"I don't see that," Clint said, "unless she knows Bat didn't do it. And if that's the case, then I want her to tell us who she thinks did do it."

"Okay," Nolan said with a shrug, "if she's in town, I'll find her."

"I'll see you here later, then."

They left the hotel together and went in separate directions.

ELEVEN

As the sheriff had advised him, the hat shop was not hard to find. It had two windows filled with hats of various shapes and colors. There was one hat that caught Clint's attention, with a sign underneath it that read, NEW FROM PARIS!

It had flowers and feathers and was unlike anything Clint had ever seen on a woman's head.

While he was still staring at it, the front door opened and a woman stepped out. She was the type to catch a man's eye immediately, starting with her red hair, then her pale skin and her full figure. Her dress covered her to the neck, but also molded itself to her body.

"I saw you looking at the hat in the window," she said. "Are you interested in buying it for your wife?"

"I'm afraid I don't have a wife."

"Your lady friend, then?"

"No lady friend right now, either," he said, "but if I did, I don't think I'd be buying her your hat from Paris."

"Oh? And why not?"

Clint got closer to her and looked her in her green eyes. "It's ridiculous."

"Really? And what expertise do you base that on? Are you an expert in women's hats?"

"Quite the contrary," Clint said. "I don't know anything about women's hats. I just know what I like, and I don't like that. Sorry."

"Oh, that's all right," she told him. "To be truthful, I don't like it much, either. But it is the latest thing, so I need to have it in my window."

"I can understand that," he said. "After all, you run a business."

She folded her arms beneath her full breasts and smiled at him. He felt a stirring inside. She was about thirty, as ripe as a woman could be, and in her prime. But he had no time for her right now. What a shame, he thought.

"So why are you looking in my window?" she asked.

"Actually," he said, "I'm looking for somebody."

"Oh? Who?"

"A fella named Lee Martin."

"Lee? His office is upstairs."

"Do you know if he's there right now?"

"I believe he is," she said. "I saw him come in this morning, and I haven't seen him leave. But his door is around the side, in the alley, so I can't be sure."

"Well," he said, "I'll go and see, then."

"Don't run off," she said. "What's your name?"

"Clint Adams."

"I'm Mandy Stuart, Mr. Adams, Tell me, if you don't need a ladies' hat, what is it you need a lawyer for? Are you in trouble?"

"No, but a friend of mine is," he said. "Mr. Martin's defending him."

"Are you referring to Bat Masterson?"

"How did you know that?"

"Well, Lee doesn't have many clients," she said. "In fact, Mr. Masterson is the only client he has right now."

"And how would you know that?" Clint asked. "Are you and Mr. Martin a couple?"

She laughed. "No, no," she said, "we're just good neighbors. We talk."

"I see," Clint said. "Well, I probably should rush and see if I can catch him."

"You do that, Mr. Adams," she said. "And when you're finished, stop into my shop. Maybe I'll show you some hats."

Clint was flustered for a moment, then said, "Maybe I'll do that."

She smiled and said, "If you do, bring some coffee," then walked back inside.

TWELVE

Clint found a stairway around the side of the building. It reminded him of other law offices he'd been to. This kind of location was cheap, and young, new lawyers were rarely able to afford anything else.

He walked up the stairs, found a shingle on the wall that read, LEE MARTIN, ATTORNEY-AT-LAW.

He knocked and then went inside.

As he expected, the office was cramped: one room with a desk, two chairs, and a file cabinet. And a handsome young man seated behind the desk. He had dark hair and looked to be all of nineteen or twenty. Clint doubted that the young man had even started shaving yet.

He looked up and smiled at Clint, obviously hoping he was a new client.

"Good morning. Can I help you, sir?"

"Don't get your hopes up," Clint said. "I'm not a new client. I'm here about the client you already have."

"Bat Masterson," Martin said. It wasn't a question. "Who are you?"

"Clint Adams."

Martin's eyes widened and his smiled broadened. It made him look even younger, almost a lad. Clint was finding it hard to believe the boy was a lawyer, but there it was behind him, on the wall: his law degree.

"The Gunsmith?"

"That's right."

"You're friends with Bat Masterson, right?"

"That's right," Clint said. "That's why I'm here."

"Well, have a seat, Mr. Adams," Martin said, half rising. "I can't offer you anything, but—"

"That's okay," Clint said. "I had breakfast. I just wanted to talk to you about Bat's defense."

"Well," Martin said, sitting back down, "his defense is he didn't do it."

"But you have to prove that, right? To a jury?"

"That's right."

"Can you do that without knowing who actually did do it?"

"Well," Martin said, "admittedly knowing who the killer is would help."

"Well, that's what I'm trying to find out," Clint said. "Have you talked to the dead man's girlfriend yet? Angie?"

"No," Martin said, "I haven't talked to her."

"Can't you find her?"

"Well, er," Martin said, "actually, I haven't looked for her."

"Why not?"

"To tell you the truth, I didn't think of talking to her. What do you think she'd know?"

"She might know if Cable Lockheart had any enemies," Clint said, "or if he'd had a fight with anyone."

"He had an argument with Bat."

"Anyone else," Clint said, impatiently. "How long have you been a lawyer, Mr. Martin?"

"I opened my office three months ago, Mr. Adams," Martin said. "I admit I'm inexperienced, but I'm a fast learner."

"I hope so," Clint said. He was glad he was in town and Bat didn't have to rely completely on this kid to bail him out of this mess. "Well, I'm going to find Angie today and see what she has to say," Clint said.

"Good," Martin said. "I hope you'll let me know if you find out anything important."

"I'll let you know everything I find out," Clint said. "I want you to have as much material as possible if you go to court."

"Why wouldn't I go to court?" Martin asked with a frown.

"Because I may prove Bat innocent before that happens," Clint said.

"Oh, right. Well, that would be good."

"Yes," Clint said, standing up, "it would."

Clint had been worried about Bat when he woke that morning. Now that he'd met his lawyer, he was even more worried. He wondered if there were any other lawyers in town with more experience whom he could talk into defending his friend.

"Where are you off to now?" Martin asked as Clint headed for the door.

"I'm going to talk to Angie," he repeated, exasperated. "Or maybe I'll go downstairs and look at some hats."

"Ah, my landlady's store," Martin said. "She's a real nice lady."

"She owns the building?"

"Yup."

"I met her on the way in."

"She's a good businesswoman," Martin said. "Owns a lot of other businesses."

"That's good to know," Clint said.

"A real nice lady," Martin said again.

"And a damned attractive one."

"Really?" Martin said. "I never noticed."

Oh boy, Clint thought, and left.

THIRTEEN

Clint went back to his hotel, hoping to find Nolan and the girl in the lobby, but when he got there the lobby was empty except for the clerk.

"Has there been anyone here looking for me today?" he asked.

"No, sir."

"Well, if anyone comes—Tom Nolan, for instance— ask them to wait here, all right?"

"Yes, sir. I will."

"Thanks."

Clint left the hotel, wondering about his next move. He decided to grab a chair and sit for a while. If nothing came to him shortly, maybe Nolan would show up with Angie.

Mason Locke and Red Cassiday were camped just outside of town.

"I don't know why we don't just ride in," Red said. "We got plenty of time."

"I ain't ready yet," Locke said. "Build us a fire, Red. I want some coffee."

"But there's hot food in town," Red said, "and hot women."

"You can get yourself a hot woman tomorrow, Red," Locke said. "Right now I want a hot fire and some hot coffee."

"Damn it, Mace—"

"Just do it," Locke said. "I promise you'll have a woman before we burn Sweetwater to the ground."

"Well, okay . . ." Red said, but as he wandered off in search of firewood he was muttering to himself.

Clint saw Tom Nolan walking toward him with a small, slender woman at his side. She had long blonde hair and pale skin.

"Mr. Adams," Nolan said, as they reached him. "This is Angie Bennett. Angie, this is Clint Adams."

"Mr. Adams," she said. "Tom says you want to talk to me?"

"Yes, about Cable Lockheart. Are you willing to talk to me?"

"Yes, sir."

Nolan got a chair for Angie and she sat down next to Clint. Nolan stood off to the side.

"You were Cable's girlfriend?"

"Yessir."

"Did you see him the night he was killed?"

"No, sir."

"Did you see him that day?"

"Yes, in the morning."

"Did you know Cable's friends?"

"He didn't have many," she said, "but yes, I did."

"Can you give me their names?"

"I know two," she said. "Jerry Dawson and Steve Kelly."

"Are they local?"

"Yes," she said, "Kelly lives in town, Dawson works on one of the ranches just outside of town."

"Okay," Clint said. "Do you know anyone who'd want to kill Cable?"

She laughed mirthlessly. "A lot of people," she said. "He's the kind of man who makes a lot of people dislike him."

"Enough to kill him?"

"Maybe," she said with a shrug.

"Do you think Bat Masterson killed him?"

"What does it matter what I think?"

"I'm just curious," he said. "Humor me."

"I don't know," she said. "Why would somebody like Bat Masterson bother to kill Cable? It wasn't like Cable had beat him at poker; it was the other way around."

"Right," Clint said. "Do you have any other boyfriends, Angie?"

"Why would you ask me that?"

"Well, a pretty girl like you," Clint said, "you must have a lot of boys after you."

"No other boyfriends," she said.

"Any boys who wanted to be your boyfriend?" he asked. "Maybe they were jealous of Cable?"

"I don't think so."

"Do you live with your parents?"

"I live alone," she said.

"Do you have a job?"

"Yes, I work in a hat shop."

"Really? The one run by Mandy Stuart?"

"Why, yes. Do you know Miss Stuart?"

"I do," Clint said. "I met her today, in fact."

"She's really nice," Angie said.

"Yes, she is," Clint said. "Okay, Angie. I don't have any other questions."

She stood up.

"If I do, can I call on you?" he asked.

"Of course," she said. "Tom knows where I live."

"Okay, thanks. Tom, why don't you walk Angie back home?"

"I have to go to work."

"Well then," Clint said, standing up, "why don't I walk you to the hat shop?"

FOURTEEN

Clint opened the door to the hat shop and allowed Angie to go in first, then followed, closing the door behind him.

"Hello, Angie," Mandy Stuart said.

"Sorry I'm a little late, Miss Stuart," Angie said. "I was talking to Mr. Adams."

"Hello Mr. Adams," Mandy said. "It's okay, Angie. Just go to work."

"Yes, ma'am."

Angie passed Mandy as the woman moved toward Clint.

"Come back to look at hats?" she asked.

"Not really."

"What, then?"

"I wanted to see you again."

She looked startled. "That's very honest of you."

"I'm an honest guy," he said.

"So where does that leave us now?" she asked.

"I thought maybe we could have dinner together."

"When?"

"Tonight?"

"Well," she said, "I close up at five. Would you like to meet me here?"

"That'd be fine," he said.

"Good. I know a place where we can go, if that's all right."

"It's your town," Clint said. "I'll see you at five."

As he headed for the door she asked, "How did it go with Lee?"

"It went okay," he said.

"Is he still representing Mr. Masterson?"

"As far as I know," Clint said. "Unless Bat fired him between now and when I saw him."

"I hope not."

Clint turned, putting his back to the door. "Um, you and he aren't—"

"No, no," she said, waving her hand, "I told you, he's just the upstairs tenant."

"That's right," he said. "He told me you're his landlady."

"Oh, he told you that?"

"Is that something you didn't want me to know?" he asked.

She shrugged. "Some men don't like businesswomen," she said. "They're threatened by them."

"Well, I don't have that problem," he said. "I'll see you at five."

After Clint left, Mandy walked over to the counter where Angie was.

"What was he questioning you about?" she asked.

"Cable's killing," Amy said. "He wanted to know who I thought killed him."

"What else?"

"If I knew any of Cable's friends."

"Did you tell him?"

"I told him about Jerry Dawson and Steve Kelly."

Mandy nodded.

"Is anything wrong?" Angie asked.

"No, nothing," Mandy said, with a smile. "I'm just curious."

"Oh."

Angie went back to what she was doing behind the counter.

Mandy said, "Angie, I'm going out for a little while. I'll be back well before closing."

"Okay," Angie said. "I'll handle everything."

"I know you will."

Mandy grabbed her shawl and put it on while she was rushing out the door.

FIFTEEN

When Clint left the hat shop, he went into the alley and climbed the stairs to Lee Martin's office. He tried the door and found it locked. He went back down to the street and headed for his hotel

Nolan had remained seated in front of Clint's hotel, waiting for him to return.

"Where are you staying?" Clint asked, sitting next to him.

"Another hotel about two blocks from here. It's called . . ." He stopped to think a minute. "Somethin' better than the Cherry Blossom, I can tell you that."

"Never mind," Clint said. "I was just curious."

"What happened with the girl?"

"She went to work," Clint said.

"You think she told you everything she knew?" Nolan asked.

"No."

"So why didn't you press her?"

"I will," Clint said. "Later. I'm going to talk to her boss first."

"Boss?"

"The lady who runs the hat shop. Mandy Stuart."

"Why?"

"She might have heard or seen something helpful, without even knowing it," he said. "I'll find out over dinner tonight. Meantime . . ." He stood up.

"Where are you going now?"

"I've got to talk to Bat, and then find his lawyer again," Clint said. "And I've got this uncomfortable feeling . . ."

"What?"

". . . that Mason Locke is not far."

"If he comes to town, you'll be able to take him, right?" Nolan asked.

"I'm hoping we won't have to find out," Clint said.

"Why?" Nolan asked, confused. "You ain't afraid, are you?"

"I'm always afraid I'll have to kill somebody, Tom," Clint said.

"But . . . you've killed so many."

"I've killed a lot," Clint said, "but only when they were trying to kill me, or someone I cared about." There were other reasons, but he didn't want to go into those now. "I'll see you later, Tom."

"Come to see your friend?" the sheriff asked when Clint entered the office.

"Yes."

Deming poured a cup of coffee and handed it to Clint. "Bring this in to him."

"Thanks."

Clint took the coffee into the cellblock and handed it through the bars to Bat.

"Thanks. What've you been up to?"

"This and that," Clint said. "I saw your lawyer. I don't have much faith in him, Bat."

"Oh, he's a good kid."

"But he's just a kid," Clint said. "You can't leave your life in his hands."

Bat sat on his cot with his coffee and grinned at Clint. "I'm not," he said. "I'm leaving my life in yours."

"I talked to Cable Lockheart's girlfriend to see if she knew of anyone who might want to kill him. Apparently, he wasn't well liked."

"Too many enemies, huh?"

"Not enemies, exactly," Clint said, "he just didn't have a lot of friends."

"What about the friends he did have?"

"I've got two names," Clint said. "I'm going to talk to them."

"Okay," Bat said. "I've got faith in you."

"Yeah, there's no pressure, right?" Clint said. "I'm going to talk to your lawyer, again."

"What about the brother, Mason Locke? Is he around?" Bat asked.

"Haven't see him, yet, but I think it's about time for him to arrive."

"Then what? You gonna sit in front of my cell with a gun?"

"If I have to," Clint said.

"You could just let me out so I can defend myself."

"Break you out, you mean?"

"I guess you could call it that."

"I think I'll keep that as my last resort, Bat," Clint said.

"That's okay," Bat said, "as long as it's on the table somewhere."

SIXTEEN

Before stopping to pick up Mandy at her store, Clint tried Lee Martin's office again and found the lawyer in.

"Came by earlier," he said.

"I was with a client."

"I thought you only had one client?"

"I got another one today," he said.

"What's the case?"

"Oh, it wouldn't interest you."

"Try me."

Martin looked embarrassed. "I have a client who is suing another man over a dog," he finally admitted.

"You're right, I'm not interested."

"Did you find the girl? What was her name? Alice?" Martin asked.

"Angie, and yes, I found her."

"What did she have to say?"

"She says she doesn't know anything."

"You don't believe her?"

"No, I don't."

"What else did she have to say?"

"I got the name of two of Cable Lockheart's friends."

"Cable had friends?" Martin pulled a pad of paper over and picked up a pencil. "Who are they?"

"Jerry Dawson and Steve Kelly," Clint said. "You know either of them?"

"No," he said, "but I'll make their acquaintance."

"I'm going to talk to them myself."

"I'll come with you."

"I can—"

"I can't just sit here in the office," Martin said, "and I can't work on another dog case. You've got to take me with you."

Clint thought it over, then said, "Okay. Tomorrow afternoon."

"Why not now?"

"Right now I have another appointment."

"Can't I come?"

"No," Clint said, "this one has nothing to do with you."

"Well, okay, then," Martin said. "Tomorrow. Where should we meet?"

"Come to my hotel, the Cherry Blossom," Clint said. "I'll let you buy me lunch."

"Um, uh," Martin stammered, "I don't have any money."

"Fine," Clint said, "I'll buy you lunch."

Clint stopped in front of the shop door and saw the CLOSED sign in the window. He tried the door, found it locked. When he knocked on the window, the door was immediately opened by Angie.

"Hello, Mr. Adams," she said. "I was just getting ready to leave."

"I'm here for Mandy," he said. "We're supposed to have dinner."

"She went out soon after you left this morning," Angie said, "and said she'd be back before closing. I'm kind of worried."

"I see. Did she say where she was going?"

"No, just that she'd be back before closing—well before closing, she said. I don't understand what could have happened to her."

"Well, don't worry," Clint said. "I'm sure it's nothing serious. If I see her, I'll let her know that you're worried."

"That's very kind of you," she said. "Thank you."

She stepped outside, then locked the door with a key.

"Do you always have a key, or did she leave it for you?" If Mandy had left it, he thought, then she knew she wasn't coming back.

"No," she said, "I have my own key."

"Would you like me to walk you home?" he asked.

"No, I'll be fine," she said. "Thank you."

He watched her walk off, wondering if he should follow her. Was there anything suspicious about Mandy not being there to meet him? Why should he think so, except that at the moment, everything made him suspicious.

He decided to go ahead and follow Angie, in the hopes that she would lead him to Mandy. If not, and there was nothing going on, it would just be the waste of a little time.

He took off after her, maintaining a sensible distance.

He followed her to a rooming house, where she went inside without ever casting a look backward. Apparently, it never occurred to her that someone might be following her.

If there was, indeed, some suspicious reason for Mandy missing their dinner appointment, it apparently had nothing to do with Angie.

He remained standing across the street from the rooming house for a few minutes, then decided to simply return to his hotel, or get something to eat, himself.

SEVENTEEN

Clint was in his room reading his favorite author, Mark Twain, when there was a knock on his door. He answered it with his gun in his hand.

"Adams," Sheriff Deming said. "Mind if I come in?"

"Sure, Sheriff," Clint said, backing away.

He walked to the bedpost and holstered his gun. The sheriff did not question why he had answered the door armed.

"What's this about?" Clint asked. "Is Bat okay?"

"Masterson is fine," Deming said. "Somebody else is dead."

"Who?"

"A woman named Mandy Suart."

"What?"

"I understand you were supposed to have dinner wiht her tonight. Did that happen?"

"No, I stopped to pick her up but she wasn't there. A girl named Angie can tell you that. She works—worked— for Mandy. What happened to her?"

"She was stabbed. Her body was found behind the livery stable."

"Did you talk to Angie?"

"Yes," the lawman said, "she backs your story. Also told me how Miss Stuart went, promising to come back before closing."

"Any idea who did it?"

"None."

"What about Bat? Ready to let him out?"

"No, why?"

"He was in a cell," Clint said. "He couldn't have killed Mandy."

"So what? Who says this killing is connected to Cable's?"

"You have a lot of murders in town?" Clint asked.

"No."

"So these two happening so close together is a coincidence?"

"Could be."

"No," Clint said, "I don't believe in coincidence."

"Can you prove the murders are connected?"

"No, I can't."

"Then until you can, Bat Masterson stays in my jail," Deming said.

"All right," Clint said, "then I'll prove it. Is there anything else I can do for you?"

"No," Deming said. "I just wanted to know if you had ever met up with Miss Stuart."

"Well, I didn't."

"That's all I needed to know. I'll be seeing you around."

"Don't you want to know where I was tonight?" Clint asked. "Or all day?"

"Why?" Deming asked. "You didn't kill her. You had no reason to."

Deming opened the door and left. Clint walked to the door and locked it.

Who had killed poor Mandy Stuart, and why? And was there any connection to the murder of Cable Lockheart?

Even though he did not believe in coincidence, what connection could be made? It wasn't as if Angie had been killed. A connection would have been easy to see in that case.

Now, in order to get Bat Masterson out of jail, it looked like Clint was going to have to solve two murders instead of one.

EIGHTEEN

Red Cassiday rolled out of his bedroll the next morning, saw Mason Locke crouched in front of the fire with a cup of coffee in his hand.

"We goin' in today?" he asked, coming up alongside his partner.

"Yeah, we're goin' in. Have a cup of coffee and then we'll go."

Cassiday poured himself a cup.

"What're we gonna do first?" he asked.

"Get a hotel room."

"And then what?"

"And then you can go and get your ashes hauled," Locke said, "or whatever you wamna do. I'm gonna go talk to the sheriff and find out how Cable got hisself killed."

"You don't want me to come with ya?"

"No," Locke said, "I don't." He tossed the remnants of his coffee into the fire. "I'll see about getting the horses saddled."

That surprised Cassiday. The job of saddling the horses always fell to him.

Mason Locke was not himself, and that was going to be bad for someone.

It always was.

Clint woke the next morning with a warm body next to him. He opened his eyes, looked at the naked form of Angie lying next to him. It took him a moment to remember how and why she was there . . .

After the sheriff had delivered the news of Mandy's death, he went back to sitting on the bed but did not pick his book back up. Instead, he stared at the wall, wondering what the hell was going on in Sweetwater.

When the second knock of the night came at the door he grabbed his gun again. This time when he opened the door he was surprised to see Angie standing there.

"Mr. Adams," she said. "Mandy is dead." She stepped forward and pressed her head to his chest. With his gun in his right hand, he put his left arm around her.

"I know," he said. "I heard. Come on in."

He drew her into the room and swung the door closed with his right hand.

"It's terrible," she said, sniffling. "When the sheriff came and told me, I couldn't believe it."

"Here, sit down," Clint said. He settled her down on the bed, then holstered his gun again.

"I'm sorry," she said. "I didn't know where else to go. First Cable, now Mandy." She looked up at Clint. "I'm frightened."

"Of what?"

"Of being killed."

He sat next to her. "Why do you think someone might want to kill you?"

"Two people who I was close to have been killed," she said. "What would you think?"

She was right. In the presence of Sheriff Deming he hadn't been able to connect the two killings, but there it was. Both victims had been close to Angie.

"What's your last name, Angie?" he asked. Maybe the answer would shed some light on the subject.

"Bennett."

Nope. It didn't help.

"Are your parents alive?"

"No, they're both dead."

"So when we talked earlier," he said, "what didn't you tell me?"

She hung her head. "I don't know what you mean."

"Sure, you do," Clint said. "There's something about Cable's death you're not telling me."

"W-what makes you say that?"

"I tend to know when somebody is lying to me," he told her. "You're lying about something."

"I'm not."

"You can't know that."

"But I do."

She took a deep breath.

"Angie, if you didn't want to tell me you wouldn't have come here, would you?"

"I don't think that's why I came here, Mr. Adams. Clint."

"Well then, why did you come?"

"I think," she said, "I came to be comforted. And to feel safe."

"Okay," Clint said, "I'll make you feel safe and then you can tell me what you're not telling me."

She leaned over and kissed him.

NINETEEN

Making her feel safe turned out to be a full night's work.

Now she was lying on her right side with her naked backside to him. The sunlight was coming through the window, landing right on her and turning the downy hair on her body into a soft glow. For such a slender girl, she had a ripe little rump. As if she knew he was watching, she wiggled then turned over onto her back. That made the sun land on her crotch, turning her blonde pubic hair into a thing of burnished gold. Her breasts were small, with pretty pink nipples.

After she'd kissed him, they had lain down together. He had only intended to hold her and make her feel comfortable, but she literally mounted him and started kissing him again. She unbuttoned his shirt, kissed his chest, and began to wriggle about on him. Before long, his cock was hard and she was rubbing up and down on it. Impatiently, she pulled off his shirt and his pants.

"Angie," he said, as she was pulling off his underwear, "this wasn't what I had in mind."

"To tell you the truth, Clint," she said, "it was what I had in mind. And, if you don't mind me saying, it looks like you have it in mind right now."

His cock was standing straight and tall . . . and hard. And there was nothing he could do to deny it.

She was down at the bottom of the bed, so she climbed up onto it and got between his legs. She took his cock in both hands, stroked it a few times, then leaned over and kissed it. He flinched and she stroked it up and down again, using both hands.

"This is the only way I think of to really feel alive," she said.

"I can't argue with that" he said.

She ducked her head and took his penis into her mouth. She bobbed up and down on it, sucking avidly, and before long he was bucking and ejaculating into her mouth.

He grabbed her, pulled her off of him, and started to pull off her clothes.

"You're not as innocent as you look," he said when she was totally naked.

"No," she said, "I'm not!"

He grabbed her, tossed her down on the bed, and buried his face in the golden hair of her crotch . . .

She moaned, bent one leg in her sleep, then moaned again as if she was having a good dream. He felt his cock start to harden as he watched her and listened. She rubbed his hands over her belly, then pushed them down to her crotch.

"You little vixen," he said. "You're awake, and you're a phony."

She opened her eyes and smiled at him. "So I'm awake," she said, "but why do you say I'm a phony?"

"Because you act like this virginal little innocent, and you're not," he said. "Your boyfriend is dead, your boss—and, I assume, friend—was killed, and you came here last night to seduce me."

"Not to seduce you," she said. "To be seduced, but you were being too nice at first, and then you were being mean."

"Mean? How?"

"By calling me a liar."

"But you are a liar."

She rolled over and reached for his cock.

"No," she said, "first you're going to tell me what you're keeping from me, and then we'll do that."

"What if I don't want to do it?"

"But I think you do."

There was no trace at all of the innocent girl who had come to his door the night before. "Bastard!"

"Start talking."

TWENTY

Angie pulled the sheet up to cover herself. Clint remained naked. He felt it gave him the upper hand.

"What do you want to know?"

"What was your relationship to Cable?"

"He was my cousin."

"Family?"

She nodded.

"Why did you not want to tell me that?"

"We didn't want anyone to know."

"Why not?" he asked again.

"It was Cable's idea. He rubbed people the wrong way. He didn't want people to dislike me because they disliked him."

"So you pretended to be his girlfriend?"

"I pretended to be the dumb girl he hung around with," she said.

"Did Mandy know the truth?"

"No."

"Anybody?"

"Cousin Mason."

"Mason Locke."

She nodded.

"Great. And he's on his way, right?"

"I would say so," she said, "as soon as he hears that Cable was killed."

"And what about Mandy?"

"What about her?"

"Who killed her?"

"I have no idea."

"Do you know anybody who'd want to hurt her?" he asked.

"No."

"And you really have no idea where she went when she left the shop?"

"No," she said, "I don't."

"Well," he said, "I guess we're just going to have to find out."

"And how do we do that?"

"Well," he said, "we can start by getting out of this bed."

She threw the sheet off and asked, "Are you sure you want to do that?"

"No, you witch, but I have to."

Her breasts were small but firm, like ripe peaches. Naked, her body was not as slender as it looked dressed. He would have liked to take more time to explore that body, but right now he was interested more in her mind. She was a liar, but how much of one? Was anything she had told him true?

"I have to get dressed," he said, tossing her shirt to her, "and so do you."

"I need a bath," she complained. "And some food."

"I can't help you with breakfast," he told her, "I have another appointment. As for the bath, you're also on your own."

She slipped on her shirt and said, "Pity."

Mason Locke and Red Cassiday rode into town while Clint and Angie were still dressing.

"How long since you been back?" Red asked.

"Not long enough."

"Where we goin' first?"

"I'm goin' to the sheriff's office," Locke said. "You go get a poke."

"You sure?"

"Git."

"Where's the nearest whorehouse?"

"I told you, it's been a while," Locke said. "Go find it yourself. Meet me at the Big Pine Saloon."

Red didn't even think to ask if Locke didn't know where the whorehouse was, how did he know there was still a Big Pine Saloon?

Locke rode over to the sheriff's office, tied off his horse, and entered without bothering to knock.

The sheriff looked up from his desk, looked shocked for a moment, then smiled. He stood up and approached Locke with his hand out.

"Hello, Mace."

"Al."

The two men shook hands. They were the same age, had grown up together in town, but taken very different paths in their lives.

"I'm sorry about Cable, Mace," Deming said.

"You still got Masterson in a cell?"

"I do."

"You gonna let me go back there and kill him?"

"I can't do that, Mace."

"How about lettin' me talk to him?"

"I'll have to take your gun."

Locke removed his gun from his holster and handed it over.

"You don't have another one, do you?" Deming asked.

Locke raised his hands to be searched. Deming patted him down quickly, then let him into the cellblock.

"Masterson," he said. "You have a visitor!"

TWENTY-ONE

Bat studied the man through the bars, instinctively knew who he was. His stomach muscles clenched, waiting for a bullet.

"Masterson," Locke said. "My name's Mason Locke. You heard of me?"

"I have."

"Cable was my brother."

"I'm sorry about that," Bat said. "I didn't kill him."

"That's not what I heard."

"Well, you heard wrong," Bat said, "like everybody else in this town."

"Can you prove you didn't do it?"

"No, I can't," Bat said. "Not from in here. But I have some people on the outside who are working on it."

"Well," Locke said, "for your sake, I hope they're good people."

"They are."

"Well," Locke said, "I'll be waitin' for you on the outside, Masterson."

"Can I talk you out of that?"

"No."

"Then I'll see you on the outside."

Locke stared at Bat, then turned and went back into the sheriff's office.

"When's the judge get here?" he asked.

"Tomorrow or the next day."

"I want to talk to him when he arrives."

"I'll tell him."

"Al, why don't you do us all a favor and get too close to Masterson's cell?"

"And let him escape?"

Locke nodded.

"I can't do that, Mace."

"That badge still means something to you, huh?" Locke asked.

"It does. Funny, huh?"

"We been friends a long time, Al," Locke said, "but don't let that badge get in my way."

"I hope it doesn't come to that, Mace."

"Me, too." He started for the door, then turned back. "Red Cassiday's in town with me."

"I don't know him."

"Well, just know that he's here, and he's with me."

"Is he going to cause trouble?"

Locke smiled and said, "I'd bet on it."

Clint let Angie take him someplace to eat. Hs still hadn't found a decent steak and eggs in town, and this was no different. The coffee was weak, too.

"I know," she said, "it's not good."

"Then why'd you bring me here?"

"It's near home," she said. "I eat here a lot."

They finished up, paid the bill, and headed for the door. Angie stepped out first, then stopped, causing Clint to bump into her.

"What is it?"

"See that man across the street? The tall one?"

"Yes," Clint said. "Looks like he's going somewhere in a hurry."

"He is," she said. She looked up at Clint over her shoulder. "He's coming to see me."

"You mean—"

"Yes," she said. "that's my cousin Mason Locke."

"You better get home then," Clint said. "You wouldn't want to disappoint him."

TWENTY-TWO

Clint walked into the sheriff's office.

"Was he here?" he asked.

From behind his desk Deming said, "You just missed him."

"He talk to Bat?"

"He did."

"You mind?"

"Go ahead," Deming said. "I haven't even locked the door yet."

Clint put his gun on the sheriff's desk and went into the cellblock.

"You just missed my guest," Bat said.

"So I heard. What did he have to say?"

"We have an appointment on the outside."

"When?"

Bat shrugged. "Whenever. What's going on?"

"Your lawyer and I are working on it. Turns out Cable's girlfriend wasn't his girlfriend, she's his cousin."

"Kissin' cousins?'

"That was just an act."

"So she's Mason Locke's cousin, too."

"Right."

"The family's all here?"

"Seems like it."

"I heard him talking with the sheriff, Clint," Bat said. "They're friends."

"Not close enough for him to let him in here with a gun, right?"

"Right," Bat said, then added, "So far."

"Does Locke have anybody else with him?"

"I don't know," Bat said. "I stopped listening. Ask the sheriff."

"I will."

"I'm supposed to see the judge in a day or two," Bat said. "It would be great if you could find out something by then."

"I'll give it my best shot, Bat."

"Yeah, I know you will," Bat said, "I'm just starting to get a bit antsy."

"I don't blame you," Clint said. "I'll be back later."

"Thanks, Clint."

Clint left the cellblock, picked his gun up off the sheriff's desk.

"Did Locke bring some men with him?" he asked Deming.

"One," Deming said, "A fella named Red Cassiday."

"Never heard of him."

"Neither have I," the lawman said. "But there's something I know about Mason Locke, Adams."

"What's that?"

"He takes care of his own business," Deming said. "If

he faced you in the street you wouldn't have to worry about being shot in the back."

"That's good to know, sheriff."

"On the other hand, Locke knows I take my badge seriously," Deming said.

"You fellas know each other well?"

"We both grew up here," Deming said. "He left town, I stayed."

"You fellas went different ways," Clint said. "How long since you've seen him?"

"A long time."

"So he may have changed."

"I don't think a man's core changes that much," Deming said.

"So we can trust that he won't try to shoot Bat in his cell?"

"He's more likely to break Masterson out and put a gun in his hand."

"Bat would prefer that." Clint headed for the door.

"Where you off to?" the lawman asked.

"I'm still trying to prove Bat innocent," Clint said. "I've got some friends of Cable's to talk to."

"You ain't plannin' on talking to Mason Locke, are you?"

"I might," Clint said. "On the other hand, he might be wanting to talk to me."

"Don't go lookin' for any trouble, Adams," Deming warned.

"I never go looking for trouble, Sheriff," Clint said.

"But somehow it manages to find you, right?" Deming asked.

"That's not my fault," Clint said. "If Locke wants to talk, I'll talk."

"I'd be careful if I was you," Deming said. "Locke's the fastest I ever saw."

"Yeah," Clint said, "you told me that before. I'll keep it in mind."

"On the other hand," Deming said as Clint opened the door, "if you two do square off, I'd like to be there to see it."

"Yeah, well, I'll make sure you get a front-row seat."

TWENTY-THREE

When Angie reached her rooming house, she saw Mason Locke sitting on the front steps.

"Been waitin' for you, cousin," he said.

"You recognize me?" she asked.

"Maybe I ain't seen you since you was little, but I sure recognize that Lockheart forehead."

Her hand immediately went to her face, but then she dropped it. She knew their fathers had both had wide foreheads, but she also knew she hadn't inherited that particular feature.

"Shut up," she said, "and come inside."

"Can't go to your room, right?"

She shook her head. "My landlady don't let me take men to my room," she said.

"Well, I don't wanna talk in the living room, so let's walk."

"Okay," she said. "Let's."

They stepped down off the porch and began to stroll.

"Do you know how it happened?" he asked.

"I only know he was found in Masterson's room," she said. "I don't know if he was killed there."

"Was he goin' to see Masterson?"

"Mace, I didn't have time to see him after the game," she said. "Masterson beat him, and I heard he left mad."

"Was he a bad loser?"

"The worst," she said.

"So he woulda went after Masterson?"

"Yes."

"Would he have bushwhacked him?"

"Yeah, he would. Cable didn't have your talent with a gun, Mace."

"But . . . he woulda shot him in the back?"

"Oh yeah."

Locke shook his head.

"Cable was Cable, Mace," she said. "Maybe he tried to ambush Masterson in his room and got killed for it."

"Masterson says no."

"Right," she said. "He says he had nothing to do with it."

"From what I've heard of Bat Masterson," he said, "if he'd killed him, he would 'fess up to it."

"Unless he ain't the man you heard he was."

"Yeah."

They walked a little farther before speaking again.

"I saw Masterson," he said.

"Where?"

"I went to the jail."

"What'd he say?"

"That he didn't do it, and he's got people tryin' to prove it."

"He's got a lawyer, but he's new and probably not so good."

"Who else?"

"Clint Adams."

Locke stopped walking.

"The Gunsmith?"

"That's right."

"He's in town?"

"Askin' questions."

"What do you know about him?"

She smiled and said, "Everythin'."

"Whaddaya mean?"

"I mean," she said, "him and me, we got real close."

"Angie—"

"I ain't a little girl anymore, Mace," she said. "Clint Adams has seen that."

Locke still stared at his cousin with a disapproving expression, then said, "Okay, so tell me everything."

They started walking again . . .

Clint stopped just outside the sheriff's office and studied the street. Mason Locke was, at that moment, probably talking with his cousin Angie.

But Angie didn't know much about what had happened in Bat's room. According to the way things had gone, she wouldn't have had time to talk with Cable before he was killed. Mason Locke wasn't going to get anything helpful out of her.

Clint wondered about Red Cassiday, and if he was as honorable as Mason Locke was supposed to be. Or if Locke was the man the sheriff remembered him being.

He stepped down into the street and crossed over to the

other side. As he did so, he saw Tom Nolan walking toward him. Nolan was not being much help, and he was
starting to get tired of the man hanging around him. Then
again, he was the one who had sent Clint the telegram.

He steeled himself to Nolan's ever-present optimism.

TWENTY-FOUR

"Clint!" Nolan shouted. "I looked for you at your hotel."

"Got out early, Tom, and had some breakfast."

"Oh," the man said, obviously disappointed, "I thought we'd have breakfast together."

"Sorry," Clint said. "Maybe tomorrow."

"We could have lunch later."

"No, I'm having lunch with Lee Martin, Bat's lawyer," Clint said.

"Great! I could come——"

"No, Tom," Clint said, "the lawyer and I have some work to do."

"Okay, but . . . did you just come out of the sheriff's office?" Nolan asked. "You see Bat?"

"Yeah, I saw him," Clint said, "and so did somebody else."

"Huh?"

"Mason Locke."

Nolan's eyes went wide. "He's in town?" he said. "And he saw Bat?"

"That's right," Clint replied, but he almost snapped, "That's what I said!"

"What happened?"

"They just had a face-to-face through the bars," Clint said. "Seems the sheriff and Locke are friends."

"You think we oughta get Bat out of there?" Nolan asked. "Break him out?"

"Break him out?" Clint asked. "That's against the law, Tom!"

"Yeah, but . . . it's you and Bat!"

"What makes you think Bat and I would break the law?" Clint asked. "I think you've got the wrong idea about who we are."

"I was just—"

"Just don't talk anymore about breaking him out of jail," Clint said. "Especially not in public."

Clint started walking away.

"Where you goin'?" Nolan asked.

"I'm going to get a drink!"

Nolan watched Clint storm away, wondering if he should follow him. Instead, he crossed the street and entered the sheriff's office.

"Clint's right, Tom," Bat said. "Don't even think about breaking me out."

"But Bat, the judge is supposed to get here today, maybe tomorrow. And Mason Locke is here."

"I know," Bat said. "I talked to him." Bat appreciated the fact that Tom Nolan had sent a telegram to Clint, getting him here. Beyond that, the man was downright annoying.

"Well, whaddaya want me to do, Bat?" Nolan asked.

"There's nothin' for you to do, Tom," Bat said. "Leave it to Clint, and to the lawyer."

"But . . . I want to help."

"I know you do, and you have," Bat said. He sat down on his cot. "There's nothin' left for you to do."

Nolan hesitated, then said, "Maybe, and maybe not."

"What do you mean—" Bat started to ask, but Nolan turned and walked out of the cellblock.

Bat just hoped the man wouldn't try anything stupid.

Mason Locke walked Angie back to her rooming house.

"Where are you gonna stay, Mace?" she asked.

"How's the old house?" he asked.

"Fallin' down."

The house Locke grew up in was outside of town. Nobody had lived there in a long time.

"Maybe I'll go out and have a look," he said.

"And your man? Cassiday?"

"I'll let him find a place in town."

"Why'd you bring him, Mace?" she asked.

"Just to watch my back, cousin," he said. "That's all."

Locke watched her walk into the building, then turned and headed back to the center of town. He decided to have a drink before doing anything else.

Clint spotted a saloon he had not been in yet called the Big Pine Saloon. He walked in and found that it was really a saloon for drinking and not much more. There were no gaming tables anywhere, and one girl working the floor even though it was early. A poker game might break out in a corner, but there was no formal gambling here.

Just drinking.

That's what he was looking for.

"Beer," he told the bartender.

"Comin' up."

The barman drew a beer with a frothy head and placed it in front of Clint.

"Just get to town?" he asked.

"No," Clint said, "I've been here a while."

"And you just got in here today?" the man asked. "Folks usually make it to the Big Pine right away. Oh, don't tell me: You're a gambler."

"Sometimes. Doesn't look like there's much of it going on here."

"Nope," the man said, "most of the gambling in town is done in other places. The Big Pine is a drinking place."

"Well," Clint said, "that's what I'm here for, right now."

"Enjoy, then. Lemme know if you need anything else. My name's Nathan."

"Thanks."

The bartender walked away. Clint looked around the Big Pine. There were about four or five men at tables, and all drinking. The girl working the floor looked bored and tired as she leaned on the far end of the bar.

Clint turned back to the bar and lingered over his beer. When he finished, he'd have to set out to find Cable Lockheart's two friends. But first, he had to pick up the lawyer at the Cherry Blossom.

TWENTY-FIVE

"No lunch?" Martin asked. "But—"

"I know, I know," Clint said. "You were looking forward to a free meal. Tell you what, we'll do that tonight. Right now, we got some work to do."

Angie had told Clint that morning where to find Jerry Dawson and Steve Kelly.

Kelly worked on a ranch outside of town. Clint figured they'd get to him first and get back to town before it got late. Then they'd talk to Steve Kelly.

"You got a horse?" Clint asked.

"Yeah, I've got one, over at the livery."

"Let's go, then."

They got to the livery and saddled up. When Martin walked his horse out, Clint saw that it was a mare of about eight or nine years old.

"That's your horse?"

"I don't ride real well, so I need something gentle," Martin admitted.

"Why don't you just use a buggy, then?"

"I do, most of the time," Martin said, "but I didn't want to slow you down."

Clint looked at the mare, who would have looked more comfortable pulling a buggy than wearing a saddle, as she was now.

"Okay," he said. "Mount up. You know where the Bar XL Ranch is?"

"I do."

"Then you lead the way," Clint said, "and we'll just travel at your pace."

Martin mounted up with some difficulty, took up the reins, and they headed off at a slow plod.

The ride to the Bar XL took two hours. Clint knew he could have done it in half that time if he'd given Eclipse his head, but he had agreed to let the lawyer go with him to talk to Cable's friends.

Maybe on the way back he'd leave the man—and the mare—behind.

When they rode up to the main house, the front door opened and two men stepped out. There were other men by the corral, who stopped working to watch.

"Help you?" one of the men asked. He was the older of the two, in his fifties, probably the owner. Clint figured the other man, ten years younger, to be the foreman.

"We're looking for Jerry Dawson."

"What for?" the man asked.

"We've got some questions for him."

"About what?"

"Cable Lockheart."

"Cable's dead," the other man said.

Clint looked at him. "You Dawson?"

"No," the man said, "I'm Dan Nesbit, foreman here."

"And I'm Xavier L. Price, owner of the Bar XL," the other man added. "Who are you?"

"This is Lee Martin," Clint said, "Bat Masterson's lawyer. My name is Clint Adams."

"Adams?" Nesbit asked.

"The Gunsmith?" Price said.

"That's right."

"You got no badge," the foreman said. "Why should we let you talk to Dawson?"

"Why not?" Clint asked. "What's it to you whether we talk to him or not? You weren't friends with Cable Lockheart, were you?"

"I couldn't stand him," Nesbit said, "but Dawson's one of my men. I don't—"

"Take it easy, Dan," Price said. "I'll take care of this."

"Okay, Mr. Price."

"I don't see any reason to keep Bat Masterson's lawyer from talking to Dawson. Go get him."

"But sir—"

"Do it!" Price said.

"Yes, sir."

"You gents want to do this inside?" Price asked them. "Out of the sun?"

"Sure," Clint said "why not?"

"Come on, then," Price said. Nesbit hadn't moved yet. "Dan, have their horses taken care of." The ranch owner looked at Clint and Martin. "They'll be ready for you when you leave."

"Okay," Clint said, "thanks."

He and Martin dismounted and followed Price up the steps. The foreman watched as they went inside, then turned and waved toward the corral for a man to come and take care of the horses.

TWENTY-SIX

Inside, Price offered the two men some cold lemonade, which they accepted. They were all holding tall glasses when Nesbit entered, with a younger man following him.

"Dawson," Price said. "This is Clint Adams, and this is Lee Martin, Bat Masterson's lawyer. They want to ask you some questions."

"Do I have to answer their questions, Mr. Price?" Dawson asked. He looked to be in his late twenties, tall, rangy, sandy-haired. He had the skin of a man who spent his days working outside.

"I'm not ordering you to answer, Dawson," Price said, "but what reason could you have for not?"

"Masterson killed Cable," Dawson said, "and Cable was my friend."

"I'll never understand why you chose to be friends with that jasper," Price said, "but it's up to you whether or not you answer questions."

Price looked at Nesbit.

"That's all, Dan."

"Yessir." Nesbit left.

"We only have a few questions, Dawson," Clint said. He didn't wait to see if the younger man was willing to answer. "Do you know of anyone who might have wanted to kill Cable?"

"Bat Masterson."

"Why?" Clint asked.

"Because he did it."

"How do you know that?"

"Everybody says so."

"Stop being an idiot, Dawson," Price said. "They're not asking you what you heard, they're asking you what you know."

"Do you know of any reason for Bat Masterson to kill Cable?" Lee Martin asked.

Dawson compressed his lips before saying, "No."

"Do you know anyone else who wanted to kill Cable?" Clint asked.

"No."

"What about Steve Kelly?"

"What about him?" Dawson asked. "He was friends with Cable."

"And with you?" Clint asked.

"Yeah, so what?"

"Would Kelly know the answers to the questions I'm asking?" Clint said.

"You'd have to ask him."

Clint walked up to Dawson and stood right in front of him. The man took an involuntary step back.

"Do you really think Bat Masterson killed Cable Lockheart?"

Dawson licked his lips nervously, then said, "I don't know."

"Do you know Mason Locke?"

"No."

"Never met him?"

"No."

"Is Locke in town?" Price asked.

"He is," Clint said.

"That's not good, Mr. Adams," Price said. "Locke is a killer."

Clint looked at Price. "You know him?"

"I knew the whole family," Price said. "The only one worth a damn is Angie."

"Look, Mr. Adams," Dawson said, "I don't know nothin'. I only know that Cable's dead."

"Do you know Mandy Stuart, who runs the hat shop?" Clint asked.

"Yeah, I met her a couple of times."

"She's dead, too," Clint said. "Any reasons somebody would want to kill Cable and her?"

"I don't know why anybody would want to kill her," Kelly said.

"Okay," Clint said. He looked at Martin. "You got any questions?"

"No."

"You can go, Dawson," Clint said.

The man looked at Price.

"Go ahead," he said. "Go back to work."

"Yessir."

Dawson left the room. Moments later, the front door closed.

"Mandy Stuart is dead?" Price asked.

"Yes."

"Why would anyone kill her?"

"You knew her?"

"Not well, but yes, I knew her. What a damn shame. What's the sheriff doing about this?"

"Not much," Martin said. "All he's doing is keeping Bat in jail."

"He's not investigating?"

"We're doing that," Martin said.

"Are you having any luck?"

"Sort of like now," Clint said. "Nobody knows anything."

"If you like," Price said, "I can get in touch with the governor, have him send somebody."

"That might not be a bad idea," Clint said. "But we'll keep asking questions."

"Very well," Price said. "I'll saddle up and come to town behind you."

"Lee," Clint sad, "you ride with Mr. Price."

"I should go with you."

"I'm going to ride hard and get back in half the time it took us to get here. You ride with Mr. Price."

"I can give him a better horse," Price said.

"Do that, but it still won't be able to keep up with mine. I'll see you both in town."

"But Clint—"

"Don't worry, son," Price said to Martin. "We'll be there soon."

Clint looked at Lee Martin, who finally nodded his agreement.

TWENTY-SEVEN

Clint made it back to town in less than an hour, turned Eclipse over to the liveryman for a good rubdown and feed.

According to Angie, Steve Kelly worked in the hardware store as a clerk. Clint walked there and entered, found a sixtyish, white-haired man behind the counter.

"Can I help you, sir?" the man asked.

"I'm looking for Steve Kelly. Does he work here?"

"He does," the man said. "He's in the storeroom, back there."

"Can I . . ."

"Sure, go ahead," the man said. "We ain't busy. My name's Walter. Tell him I said it's okay."

Clint started for the back, then stopped.

"Why are you letting me go back there?" Clint asked. "You don't even know me."

"You're the Gunsmith," Walter said. "In my store. I'm honored, sir."

"Well . . . thanks, Walter."

He went into the storeroom, found a young man moving sacks of flour and grain.

"Steve Kelly?"

The young man turned, frowned at Clint. He was the same age as Jerry Dawson but built with more muscles—probably from moving sacks like the ones he was moving at that moment.

"I'm Kelly," he said, straightening up. "What can I do for you?"

"I'd like to ask you a few questions," Clint said, "about Cable Lockheart."

"Cable's dead," Kelly said. "Bat Masterson killed him."

"That's what I want to talk to you about," Clint said. "Do you know anyone else, other than Bat Masterson, who might have wanted to kill him?"

"No, why?" Kelly asked. "Who says Masterson didn't do it?"

"I do."

"And who are you?"

"My name's Clint Adams."

Kelly looked shocked. "The Gunsmith?"

"That's right."

Kelly looked around, as if seeking an escape route.

"Relax," Clint said, "I'm only here to ask some questions."

"What for? To try to save Bat Masterson?"

"Bat didn't kill Cable," Clint said, "but the only way to prove it is for me to find out who did."

"What if you end up proving he actually did it?" Kelly asked.

"Then he'll have to pay for it."

"Okay," Kelly said, "go ahead, ask your questions."

He asked Kelly the same questions he'd asked Dawson.

"I'm sorry," Kelly said, "I can't point you to one or two people who might have wanted to kill Cable."

"How about ten? Or twenty?"

Kelly grinned. "Okay, so Cable wasn't well liked. That don't mean the people who didn't like him wanted to kill him."

"No, you're right, it doesn't mean that," Clint said. "Thanks for talking to me, Mr. Kelly."

"Look," Kelly said, as Clint started to leave. "I want whoever killed Cable to pay. For your sake, I hope it's not your friend."

"Thanks," Clint said, and left the storeroom.

TWENTY-EIGHT

Out front, Clint stopped once again to talk to Walter.

"How'd it go?" the older man asked.

"It went fine," Clint said. "You mind if I ask you a question?"

"Sure," Walter said, leaning on the counter, "go ahead."

"How did you know who I was when I walked in?"

"I was in Abilene ten years ago."

"That's funny," Clint said. "So was I."

"I was wearin' a badge," Walter said.

Clint took a closer look at the man, past the wrinkles, past the white stubble on his jaws.

"Marshal Walt Rayland?"

"Once upon a time," Walter said. "Now I'm Walter Ray, store owner."

"How long?"

"'Bout eight years," Walter said. "After you left Abilene, I lasted about another six months, decided I was too old and the badge was getting too heavy. Drifted for about a year and a half, then decided I was too old for that. Settled here."

"You like it?"

Walter shrugged. "I'm doin' okay."

"You know why I'm in town?"

"Got a feelin' it's about Bat Masterson and Cable Lockheart," Walter said, "considerin' Steve was friends with that asshole Cable."

"That's right. You got any idea who might have killed him?"

"Figurin' Masterson didn't?" Walter asked. "I can't help you. I know a few men who wouldn't piss on him if he was on fire, but no one who would kill him."

"Okay," Clint said. "Thanks."

"You know you're gonna have to deal with Mason Locke, right?"

"He's already in town, and he's already had a talk with Bat."

"And you?"

"Not yet."

"Man like Locke, maybe he won't talk to you first," Walter said. "He might just come after you."

"I know that, too," Clint said, "but I've been told he'll come alone."

"I wouldn't count on that," Walter said. "You'd be smart to get somebody to watch your back."

"The only man in town I'd trust to do that is in jail," Clint said, "so I guess I'll have to go it alone." He started for the door.

"Clint?" Walter reached under the counter, brought out his gun and holster, the belt wrapped around it.

"I keep this under here in case I get robbed," he said. "Haven't worn it in year, but if you need me—"

"Why would you do that, Walter?"

"If I remember right," Walter said, "you saved my life in Abilene."

"You don't owe me anything."

"Maybe you feel that way," Walter said, "but I don't. So you just say the word—"

"Put the gun away, Walter," Clint said. "I appreciate the offer and I'll keep it in mind."

"Okay," Walter said. He put the gun back under the counter. "Okay."

Clint touched the brim of his hat and said, "Nice to see you again, Walter," and left.

TWENTY-NINE

Clint went back to the Big Pine Saloon for a beer, drank it standing by the bat wing doors. He was standing there when Lee Martin finally rode into town with X.L. Price. Seeing them, he stepped outside. They rode up to him and stopped.

"Buy you gents a beer?"

"Don't mind if I do," Price said, "but this place is a dump."

Martin got off his horse—a tough looking steeldust—and walked gingerly into the saloon.

"How'd you like ridin' a real horse?" Price asked him.

"I think I'll stick to the horse and buggy from now on," Martin said.

They joined Clint at the bar. There were still about half a dozen others in the bar, just sitting and drinking. The girl leaning on the bar was a different one, but she had the same bored, tired look.

"Beers for my friends, and another for me," Clint said to the bartender.

"You talk to Dawson?" Martin asked.

"Yeah," Clint said, "he had the same answers Kelly did."

"So no help."

"No."

The bartender laid out three beers.

"Nice to see you in my place, Mr. Price," he said.

Price just nodded, sipped the beer, and made a face. He put it back down on the bar.

"I guess I'll go and see the Sheriff," he said. "and I should probably talk to the Mayor."

"I thought you were going to notify the Governor?" Martin asked.

"Well, I have to talk to them first," Price said, "and the Judge, if he's here, yet." He looked at Clint. "You understand, right?"

"Sure," Clint said, "sure I do, Mr. Price."

"I'll see you gents later," Price said, and walked out.

"Is he really going to get in touch with the Governor?" Martin asked.

"I doubt it," Clint said. "He didn't ask where he could get hold of us."

"So? Why did he say he would?"

Clint shrugged.

"Something's going on, Lee," Clint said.

"Like what?"

"Politics, maybe," Clint said. "Otherwise, why would he want to talk to the Mayor? What's the Mayor like?"

"As you say," Martin answered, "a politician."

Clint shook his head.

"I don't know what's going on," he said.

"But you're gonna find out, right?"

"I'm going to try."

The bartender came over.

"Mr. Price say what was wrong with the beer?" he asked.

"He likes lemonade, apparently," Clint said.

The batwing doors opened and a man walked in.

"Uh-oh," the bartender said.

Clint saw the man in the mirror behind the bar.

"Who is he?" Clint asked.

"Mason Locke," the bartender said. "Ain't seen him in years, but that's him."

Clint looked at Lee Martin, who suddenly looked very nervous.

"Take it easy."

"What if he sees us?"

"He doesn't know you, does he?" Clint asked.

"No, but . . . what about you?"

"We've never seen each other," Clint said, "but I am going to have to talk to him, so as soon as he settles at a table, or at the bar, you leave."

Martin almost bolted at that moment, but Clint said, "Wait! And then walk."

Martin nodded jerkily.

Mason Locke seemed to be looking for someone. When he didn't find who he was looking for he walked to the bar.

"Beer," he said.

Lee Martin left the bar and walked out, moving way too fast.

Locke turned and looked after him, then eyed Clint.

"Somethin' I said?"

"He just has some work to do."

The bartender brought Locke his beer.

"Mason Locke, right?" Clint asked.

Locke sipped his beer.

"What's it to you?"

"I think you and I have some interests in common."

Locke studied Clint a little closer, then sipped his beer again.

"Adams, right?"

"How'd you guess."

"Nobody else in this town would talk to me," Locke said.

"Can we talk?"

"You gonna tell me Masterson's innocent?"

"Yup."

"Then I'm gonna ask you to prove it to me."

"That's what I'm trying to do," Clint said, "but I need a little time."

"You don't need the time from me," Locke said. "You need it from the Judge."

"Is he here?"

Locke nodded.

"Rode in earlier today," he said. "You been out of town?"

"A few hours, yeah."

"Must've been then," Locke said. "I heard Masterson's goin' to court in the mornin'."

Crap. Clint thought.

"So you better talk to him," Locke said. "You know Judge Reilly?"

"No."

"Not an easy man," Locke said.

"Guess I better track him down." Clint put his mug down. "I heard you brought somebody to town with you?"

"Adams," Locke said. "You got nothin' to worry about

from me if you prove Masterson innocent. All I want is whoever killed my brother. You gimme that and we'll be okay."

"Then that's what I'll do," Clint said.

Locke lifted is mug to Clint, who turned and walked out.

THIRTY

When Clint left the Big Pine he was thinking maybe Mason Locke was not going to be such a big problem. According to Locke himself, the Judge was going to be Clint's biggest concern.

Judge Reilly. The name meant nothing to him. But three people in town he could ask—the Sheriff, Lee Martin, and Walter Ray.

It wouldn't hurt to have three opinions on the Judge before he actually spoke with him.

The Sheriff first.

"Another visit with Masterson?" Deming asked when Clint entered.

"No," Clint said, "I heard the Judge arrived."

"Just this afternoon," Deming said. "I'll be taking Masterson into his courtroom in the morning."

"Judge Reilly, is it?"

"That's right," Deming said. "Judge Rupert Reilly. How did you hear?"

"Mason Locke told me."

"You talked to Locke already?"

"Yes."

"And no shots fired?"

"He wasn't anxious to exchange shots," Clint said. "Neither was I. Apparently, we both have other concerns."

"Like what?"

"Finding his brother's real killer."

"Sounds like you two had a nice long talk."

"Not so long, but pretty good."

"You got him talked into believing Masterson didn't kill Cable?"

"No, not quite," Clint said, "but he's willing to give me time to prove it."

"Time's not up to him to give," Deming said.

"I know, it's up to the Judge," Clint said. "That's why I want to talk to him, but first I wanted you to tell me about him."

"He's a hard man," Deming said. "Law and Order man all the way. You won't be able to put anything over on him."

"I don't want to pull anything over on him," Clint said. "I just want a fair shake for Bat."

"Well, good luck, that's all I gotta say."

"Thanks," Clint said, even though he knew the man was being sarcastic. "Will I find him in the courthouse?"

"Either there or at his hotel."

"Where's he stay when he's in town?"

"Just by coincidence, your hotel."

"That'll be convenient."

Clint headed for the door, then stopped and turned.

"Any word on who killed Mandy Stuart?"

"Nothin'," Deming said. "I ain't no damn detective, either. But don't worry, I'll find him. I got somethin' I never told nobody."

"What's that?"

Deming eyed Clint, then seemed to decide to confide in him. "She was strangled with an orange scarf she was wearin'. Pulled so tight that her tongue was stickin' out. Poor girl."

"I'll keep my ears open," Clint said.

"Yeah," Deming said, "thanks."

Clint found Martin sitting behind his desk. The hat shop downstairs was closed.

"I didn't hear any shots," Martin said, as Clint walked in.

"There weren't any," Clint said.

"What happened?"

"We talked," Clint said. "He told me Judge Reilly was in town."

"Reilly," Martin said. "That's not good. I was hoping for Judge Franks."

"What's wrong with Reilly?"

"No wiggle room with him," Martin said. "He's a stickler for the law."

"That's good," Clint said. "If there's no evidence against Bat he can't convict him."

"Judge Reilly's got his own ideas about evidence," Martin said. "We need to prove Bat didn't do it."

"Okay," Clint said. "Did you get word when to be in court?"

"Just had a messenger," Martin said. "Nine a.m."

"I'll see you there, then."

"Where are you going now?"

"I'm going to make one more stop, and then I'm going to talk to the Judge."

"Should I come with—"

"No!" Clint said, and went out the door.

"Back so soon?" Walter asked. "You here for me or Jerry?"

"You, Walt, but just to ask you a question."

"Shoot."

"Judge Rupert Reilly."

"Hard man."

"That's what I'm hearing."

"You're gonna have to show him a killer, Clint," Walter said.

"Well," Clint said, "if that's what I have to do, but first I'll try talking to him."

"Well, try to catch him at the courthouse," Walter said. "Don't bother him while he's eating. He hates that."

"Thanks for the advice."

He started to leave, then turned.

"Walt, what can you tell me about E.L. Price?" he asked.

"He's a snake," Walter said. "Don't trust him."

"Really? He seemed real eager to cooperate when we went out to his ranch to talk to his man Kelly."

"You never know what Price is thinking, Clint, but I can tell you it ain't good. What'd he tell you?"

"He said he'd notify the Governor to send someone in to investigate, but I didn't really believe him."

"Then you're a good judge of character," Walter said. "Price won't do anything unless it profits him."

"Then how does it profit him to lie to me about that?" Clint asked.

"I don't know," Walter said. "You could ask him, but he'd probably lie to you."

"Thanks for the advice," Clint said.

"I'll tell you somethin' else, Clint," the ex-lawman said.

"What's that?"

"You ain't gonna get Bat out of this mess unless you march the real killer right into court."

"Well," Clint said, with a shrug, "if that's what it takes."

Clint was out the door and already heading away when Walter opened it and stuck his head out.

"Hey, one more thing!"

"What's that?"

"Keep in mind that the Judge is notoriously cheap."

"Thanks," Clint said. "Maybe that'll be helpful."

THIRTY-ONE

Clint walked to the courthouse, hoping he hadn't wasted too much time talking to everyone else. He entered the two story building and practically ran into an older man wearing a black suit and looking every inch a judge.

"Judge Reilly?"

The man stopped short, looked Clint up and down, then said, "I'm on my way out, young man. You can see me tomorrow."

"I really need to talk to you now, Judge."

"I'm going to have dinner," the Judge said.

"Good, I'll come with you."

"I eat alone, sir!" the Judge said, sternly.

The man started away and Clint shouted, "How about if I pay?"

The Judge stopped.

"The biggest, thickest steak you can find," Clint said.

The Judge turned and looked at him.

"What's your name?"

"Clint Adams."

"*The* Clint Adams?" the older man asked.

"Yes, sir."

"And you want to talk to me about what?"

"Bat Masterson."

The Judge studied Clint for a few moments, then said, "Come along, Mr. Adams. This just might prove interesting."

The Judge picked the most expensive restaurant in town. Clint was happy to find it was also the best, and that was just based on the coffee.

They ordered two steak dinners and enjoyed the coffee while they waited.

"Let's try and get this out of the way before the food comes," Reilly said. "I truly hate discussing business while I eat."

"I don't blame you, sir."

"And stop the 'sir' stuff," the older man said. "Just call me Judge."

"Yes, sir . . . Judge."

Reilly had snow white hair and sky blue eyes. His face was covered with wrinkles he might have earned in sixty-five or seventy years.

"You want to convince me that your friend, Masterson, is innocent, right?"

"Yes, si—Judge, I do, but I want to do it by bringing you the real killer."

"Good," Reilly said. "Bring him to court tomorrow morning. And a confession would be nice."

"I could probably do it with a little more time, Judge."

"Time is something I can't give," Reilly said. "I have other towns to visit. I'll be hearing the case in the morning, and ruling on it in the afternoon."

"Just like that? No jury? No trial?"

"Tomorrow is the trial, Mr. Adams," Reilly said. "The trial of Bat Masterson. I never thought I'd be the one to put him on trial, but it had to happen some time."

"Why's that?"

"You of all people know that," Reilly said. "You can't flout the law with a gun forever and get away with it. It'll happen to you, too, eventually. It will happen to all of you."

"Is that what you really think?" Clint asked. "It'll happen to all of us?"

"It is."

"And how many of 'us' have you had in your court, so far?"

"None, until now," Reilly said. "Bat Masterson will be my first."

"And you intend to make an example of him?"

"I do," Reilly said, "unless you march the real killer into my court, as you say you can."

"Then I guess that's what I'll have to do," Clint said, standing up.

"Are you leaving?"

"I am."

"But you said you'd pay."

Clint dug into his pocket, dropped some money on the table.

"That should pay for both meals," he said. "Choke on both of them."

"Wait just a minute—"

"Sorry, Judge," Clint said, "but I've had about as much of you as I can stomach."

"How dare you—" the Judge started to say around a mouthful of beef, but Clint was already heading for the door.

THIRTY-TWO

Clint had succeeded in making sure the Judge was against not only Bat, but him. Apparently, the juror had it in for men with reputations, and was only too happy to find Bat Masterson in his court room.

Clint left the restaurant thinking that maybe the thing to do was break Bat out.

He was also still hungry.

He had not yet eaten in the Cherry Blossom's small diningroom, so he returned to his hotel and got himself a table away from the doors and windows. It was dinner time, and most of the tables were taken. He probably should have found Tom Nolan and taken him to dinner, but the man was just too annoying.

He had just been served his steak dinner—which did not look as good as the one he'd walked away from—when Angie walked in. She looked around the room, spotted him, and hurried over.

"Hungry?" he asked.

"I ate," she said, seating herself, "but I wouldn't say no to a piece of pie and some coffee."

Clint called the waiter over and Angie ordered apple pie and coffee.

"I heard you and cousin Mason had a talk," she said.

"We did," Clint said. "He seems like a sensible man."

"Really?" she asked. "That's not the word I'd use for him."

"Well, maybe he was pulling the wool over my eyes, but he seemed to genuinely want to find his brother's killer. The real killer."

"Well, he's still pretty convinced it's Bat Masterson," Angie said.

"Bat goes to court tomorrow, and the Judge has it in for him because he has a reputation," Clint said. "So if your cousin still has it in for him, it looks like Bat's in trouble."

"A trial should go on for a while, shouldn't it?" she asked.

"Normally," Clint said, "but I had a talk with the judge. He seems intent on having a one day trial."

"Then you don't have much time."

"Angie," he asked, "why don't you think Bat did it?"

"I just don't see why he would," she said. "He beat Cable for all his money."

"But what if Cable was waiting for him in his room?" Clint asked. "And Bat killed him in self defense?"

"Then he would've used his own gun, right?"

"Yes, but you seem to be the only one smart enough to think that."

The waiter came with her pie and coffee, another beer for Clint.

"So what are you gonna do?" she asked.

"Do you know the man your cousin brought with him? Cassiday?"

"No, I never met him."

"Would your cousin use a backshooter if he faced me or Bat?"

"Mason would want to take you on his own," she said.

"Are you sure of that?"

"Positive."

Clint wondered if he could trust everything she was telling him? After all, he was dealing with her family.

"You can trust what I tell you, Clint," she said, as if reading her mind. "Don't trust Mason to be patient, but he won't try to bushwack you."

"Okay," he said, pushing his plate away. "That pie looks good, I think I'll have some."

THIRTY-THREE

Red Cassiday had spent the entire afternoon at one of Sweetwater's two whorehouses. He stayed because he was also able to get food there. Food, and a lanky redhead who fit his penchant for lean women with long legs and flat chests.

And a talented mouth.

She had his cock in her mouth just then, as he looked down at her bobbing red tresses. She sucked him wetly, moaning eagerly as she rode his long cock with her wide mouth. Every so often she brought her head down, taking the entire length inside, and staying there, shaking her head, playing with his balls with one hand, until she finally came up for air, gasping.

"You have a beautiful big cock, Red," she told him.

Too bad, she thought, you smell so bad. Least he could have done before coming to the whorehouse was take a bath. Still, he seemed to have money to throw around, and he was throwing it all her way, which suited her.

"God, when you do that it makes me feel like my head's gonna come off," he told her.

"You think that was good?" she asked. She turned around, got on all fours and lifted her ass in the air so he could see her wet, pink pussy. "Try this."

"Oh yeahhhhh," he said, getting to his knees behind her . . .

Red was finally able to pull himself away from the redhead—he didn't remember her name—and headed over to the Big Pine saloon to meet Locke and find out what was going on.

Mason Locke, after talking with Clint Adams in the saloon, went and took care of his horse, then got himself a room and a bath. Following that he'd gotten himself a meal, eating at a bad restaurant his cousin Angie had recommended. By the time Red Cassiday entered the Big Pine Saloon Locke was feeling refreshed.

"You been fuckin' yourself stupid all day?" Locke asked.

"You bet!"

"Get my friend a beer," Locke told the bartender.

"Comin' up."

"You eat?" Locke asked.

"Yeah, at the whorehouse."

"Sounds like your kind of place."

"What's been goin' on?"

"Masterson's going to court in the mornin'," Locke said.

"We lettin' him get there?"

"I know the Judge," Locke said. "He'll most likely convict him in one day."

"Then what?"

"Then he'll send him to prison."

"Where?"

"It don't matter," Locke said. "He's never gonna get there."

"Okay, sounds good."

"There's only one problem."

"What's that?"

"Clint Adams."

Red's eyes went wide.

"The Gunsmith's in town?"

"Yeah, and he's determined to prove Masterson didn't kill Cable."

"Jesus," Red said, "we gotta go through him to get to Masterson?"

"That's right."

"You got a plan?"

Mason Locke nodded and said, "I got a plan."

Clint didn't know what he could get done after dark. He was no closer to finding Cable Lockheart's killer than he was when he started. Bat was walking into Reilly's court in the morning, and would probably walk out convicted of murder.

At that point Clint would have to do something drastic. Unless he had something done before that. He had to make sure Lee Martin drew the case out so that he'd have all day to work on a plan.

Maybe he could still catch Martin in his office before he went back to his hotel. If not, he didn't know where the young lawyer lived.

He walked Angie out of his hotel.

"What are you gonna do?" she asked.

"I have to talk to Bat's lawyer, again."

"Maybe I can talk to Mason and find out what's really on his mind."

"That would be helpful?"

"Can I come to your room later?" she asked.

He smiled and said, "That would be helpful, too."

THIRTY-FOUR

When Clint entered Lee Martin's office he found the man asleep on top of his desk. Martin jerked awake, hurriedly moved from the desk to the chair.

"You're living here?"

Martin cleared his throat, then used both hands to rub his face.

"Just until I can afford to get a room somewhere," he said. "It's okay, really. I'm able to work late. I'll have my defense ready for tomorrow."

"What is your defense?"

"It's simple," Martin said. "There's no proof Bat shot Cable."

"That may not matter."

"What do you mean?"

Clint told Martin about his talk to Judge Reilly, and the Judge's response.

"It seems to me he wants to find Bat guilty."

"That's not only unfair, it's unprofessional," Martin said.

"I agree."

"What happened with Mr. Price contacting the Governor?"

"I don't know," Clint said. "I haven't seen him since the two of you arrived in town."

"What are you going to do?"

"I have two options," Clint said. "I'll have to find the real killer tomorrow, or break Bat out to save him. Either way I'll need your help."

"I can't help you break a man out of jail," the young lawyer said.

"I know that," Clint said. "What I need you to do is keep the trial going, make it last. If you could get the trial to go to a second day—"

"I understand," Martin said. "As much as the Judge will be trying to finish in one day, I have to try to extend the trial."

"Just until I can figure something out."

"Okay," Martin said. "I'll do my best."

"I know you will," Clint said. "Would you like me to get you a hotel room for the night?"

"Thanks, but no," Martin said. "I'd actually prefer to stay here tonight."

"All right," Clint said. "If you change your mind, let me know."

"I will. Thanks."

"Good-night," Clint said, and left.

THIRTY-FIVE

"Are you goin' to him?"

Angie was coming down the steps from the front door of the rooming house. She turned quickly and saw her cousin standing there.

"You surprised me," she said.

"Are you goin' to his hotel?" Locke asked, again. "To be with him?"

"Yes."

"Why?"

"Because he makes me feel like no other man has ever made me feel," she said.

"And?"

"And to find out what he's plannin' for tomorrow."

Locke came close to her, touched her hair.

"So, you're not in love with him?"

"Of course not!" she said.

"You know," he said, "of all our family, it's now down to just you and me, Angie."

"I know that, Mace."

He took hold of her by her upper arms, squeezing tight.

"You're hurtin' me."

"Just remember where your loyalties lie," he said to her.

"I remember, Mace," she said. "How could I forget?"

He released her, and she rubbed herself where he had gripped her.

"Just see that you do," he said, and let her go on her way.

Clint was in his room, considering his options for the next day, when the knock came at his door. He expected it to be Angie, but took his gun to the door, anyway. It was her. She looked at the gun in surprise.

"You're a very careful man," she said.

"It's why I'm still alive."

He let her in, closed the door, and holstered the gun, left it hanging on the bedpost.

"Did you talk to the lawyer?" she asked, sitting on the bed.

"Yes," Clint said. "He's going to stall the trial as long as he can."

"What will that accomplish?"

"Hopefully, I can find the killer."

"And if you can't?"

"I don't know, Angie," Clint said. "I'd hate to have to break Bat out of jail. Neither one of us wants to break the law."

"But if you have to?"

"I don't know," he said. "That would put both of us on the run. Not only from the law, but probably from your cousin."

"Have you ever been on the run?" she asked.

"Not from the law," he said. "Not as a wanted criminal."

He sat down next to her and she touched his arm.

"I'm sorry you're havin' this trouble."

He looked at her.

"I'm sorry you lost your cousin."

He leaned over and kissed her. She responded, opening her mouth to him, sliding her tongue inside. He worked on the buttons of her shirt, removed it and tossed it away. He caressed her naked breasts, her nipples coming to life beneath his fingers . . .

Red Cassiday didn't know why he had to stand outside Clint Adams' hotel all night. Yeah, he did. It was because Mason Locke told him to.

Locke wanted to know how long Angie stayed with Adams, and when she left the hotel. He told Red it didn't matter if it took all night.

"Ah, hell, Mace," Red said, "I was hopin' to go back to the whorehouse tonight."

"Do you even have a hotel room?" Locke asked him.

"No."

"Did you think they'd let you stay in the whorehouse all night?"

"Well—"

"Just do what I tell you," Locke said. "Everythin' always goes better that way, don't it?"

And actually, it did, so Red decided to stop sulking and keep watch across the street from the hotel, like he was told.

He rolled a cigarette and lit it.

* * *

Angie fell asleep as soon as they had finished making love. Clint slipped naked from the bed and looked out the window. Across the street he saw the glowing tip of a cigarette.

He looked back at the bed. Angie was lying on her back with the sheet covering her breasts, but her arms on top. Clint could clearly see the bruises forming on her upper arms where someone had grabbed her. It could only have been Mason Locke.

Clint was sure her cousin had grabbed her and held her tight while giving her instructions. And he'd probably also given instructions to the man across the street, smoking in the dark.

Angie had no weapons on her. He'd made sure of that the best way he knew how. She could have grabbed his gun from his holster, but he doubted her instructions included that. It was more likely she'd only been told to find out what his plans were.

The man across the street had to be Red Cassiday. If his instructions were to watch, then there was nothing to worry about.

Just to be sure, Clint grabbed the straight backed wooden chair by the window and quietly jammed it beneath the doorknob. Nobody would be able to get into the room without raising a ruckus. He went back to bed, lying next to Angie with the gun hanging close by.

THIRTY-SIX

Clint woke in the morning when Angie stirred, entwining her legs with his.

"'mornin'," she said.

"Good morning."

She looked at the window.

"It's early."

"Yes," he said. "I have to get started."

"Can you buy me breakfast?"

"Downstairs," he said. "Then I have to get moving."

"Do you know what you're gonna do?"

"I have an idea."

"What?"

"Let's talk about it over breakfast."

"All right."

"I'll get dressed quickly," he said, "and meet you downstairs. I'll only use a little of the water in the pitcher.

"All right."

* * *

When Clint got down to the lobby he walked first to the front door, looked out across the street. The man he thought was Red Cassiday must have been dozing, because he didn't move, even though he was standing. Clint wondered if he'd been charged with following him, or Angie?

He turned and went into the diningroom.

"Alone, sir?" A waiter asked.

"No, there's two of us. Something away from the door and windows."

"Yes, sir, follow me."

He sat and ordered a pot of coffee right away.

"When the lady arrives you can bring us both steak-and-eggs."

"Biscuits?"

"Of course."

"Comin' up, sir."

The waiter left and Clint poured himself a cup of coffee. He nursed it until Angie arrived, then poured her a cup.

"Red Cassiday is across the street," he told her.

"Who?"

"I thought we weren't going to lie to each other, Angie," he said. "He's your cousin's friend."

"Oh, him. What's he doin' there?"

"He was there all night," Clint said. "He's either going to follow you when you leave, or me."

"Why?"

"You'd have to ask your cousin that," he said.

"I will."

The waiter came over with their breakfasts. Angie actually clapped her hands and then dug in.

* * *

Clint decided to leave the hotel at the same time as Angie.

"Is that him?" she asked.

"Yes," he said, "he's still dozing."

"While standin'?"

"Well, he's been there all night," Clint said. "We better wake him so he doesn't get into trouble with your cousin, Mason."

"That's nice of you."

"Let's see if he thinks so."

They crossed over and approached the man, who was now beginning to list to one side with his eyes still closed.

"Should we wake him?" she asked, in a low voice.

"Wait," Clint said. He reached over and plucked the man's gun from his holster. "Now."

"How?" she asked. "Touch him?"

"Like this." Clint poked the man in the shoulder and said, "Hey!"

Red Cassiday's eyes snapped open and he immediately went for his gun, only to find his holster empty.

"What the—"

"Hello, Red."

Cassiday stared at Clint, then looked at the girl.

"You know who this young lady is, don't you?" Clint asked.

"Um, yeah, Angie."

"And me?"

"Adams," Cassiday said.

"You were asleep on the job, Red."

"Huh?"

"You've been out here all night, but this morning you were asleep."

"Asleep?" Red asked. "Standin' up? That's—"

"That's what you were doin', Red," Angie said. "Do you want Mason to know you fell asleep?"

"Um, uh, well, no . . ."

"Here," Clint said, handing him back his gun. "Put that back in your holster."

Red took the gun and holstered it.

"We took that from you while you were asleep," Angie said.

Red just stared at her.

"Mason doesn't have to know, Red," Clint said.

"You won't tell him?" Red asked.

"Well, that depends."

"On what?"

"On what you're doing here in the first place."

"I, um, I'm supposed to watch her."

"Her?"

"The girl," Red said. "Angie."

"Why?"

"I don't know," Red said. "All I know is I'm supposed to watch her, tell Mason when she leaves the hotel."

"You're not supposed to follow me?" Clint asked.

"You? Uh, no—"

"Or Angie."

"Um, not follow her, just . . . ya know, keep an eye on her."

"I see," Clint said. "Make sure she's safe, that kind of thing?"

"Uh, yeah."

"Okay, Red," Clint said. "She just left, and she's safe. She's heading home, now."

"Um, okay."

"You want to know where I'm going?"

"Um . . ."

"I'm on my way to the jail," Clint said. "You can tell Mason that."

Clint turned to Angie and said, "I'll see you later. You can tell your cousin anything I've told you."

"What? I wasn't—"

"You don't want to make him mad," Clint said. "Just tell him. Or he may put some more bruises on your arms."

She touched her arms and stared at him.

Clint nodded at Red, who was still so stunned by recent events he simply nodded back.

THIRTY-SEVEN

Clint went directly to the Sheriff's office. It was eight a.m. so he had an hour before Bat was to go to court.

"No time, Adams," Deming said as he entered. "I have to take him to court."

"In an hour," Clint said. "I need to talk to him first."

Deming sighed loudly.

"All right. Go ahead.

Clint entered the cellblock, saw that Bat had donned his jacket and tie, tried to make himself respectable even though his shirt was now grimy.

"You need a new shirt."

"Can you get me one in the next hour?" Bat asked.

"Probably not."

"What's going on?"

Clint moved close to the cell. Bat did the same. They both lowered their voices.

"Bat, I may have to break you out."

"I thought that was a last resort."

"It is."

"That bad?" Bat asked.

"It's the Judge," Clint said. "Seems he relishes the idea of putting Bat Masterson behind bars."

"Just my luck."

"Look, I've talked to Lee. I told him to stall as long as possible. But if I can't find the real killer by the end of the day, you and me are going to have to take it on the lam."

"Well," Bat said, "my horse is at the livery stable."

"You're willing?"

"To become an outlaw with my good friend the Gunsmith? Why not. Sounds like fun."

"Bat—"

"I know, Clint," he said, "but I'm not willing to die just so I don't sully my name. You don't have to come with me, though. Just get me a gun."

"Forget that," Clint said. "If you're going, I'm going, too. But we still have the rest of the day."

"Well then, you better get busy," Bat said. "I'll do what I can to help young Martin drag it out. What's the judge's name?"

"Reilly."

"Okay," Bat said, "let's see how much of a thorn I can be in Judge Reilly's side."

"If I know you," Clint said, "you'll be a giant pain."

THIRTY-EIGHT

Clint left the jailhouse, starting to feel sorry he had convinced Bat to put his life in his hands. He probably should have sent for Talbot Roper right away. The best private detective in the country probably would have had the killer in custody by now.

Bat's plan when he left the poker game that morning had been to get some sleep and then have some lunch. But according to him, when he arrived at his hotel he'd decided to have breakfast first. Coincidentally, he had been staying in the Cherry Blossom Hotel, where Clint was staying.

Clint went to the Cherry Blossom and grabbed the waiter who had served he and Angie that morning.

"Were you working the morning Bat Masterson was arrested?" he asked.

"Uh, no, sir. I remember that morning, though. Mr. Masterson stopped here for breakfast, first."

"That's right. Who waited on him?"

"I believe it was Kenny, sir."

"Is he here today?"

The man looked around, then said, "Yes, sir. He's waiting on that far table right now."

Clint looked and saw a thirtyish, portly man with thinning hair talking to a man and woman at a table.

"Okay, thanks."

Clint positioned himself so that Kenny the waiter would have to go past him to get to the kitchen.

"Kenny?"

The man turned his head and looked at Clint pleasantly.

"Sir?"

"I need to talk to you."

"I'm waiting on two tables right now, sir," the man said.

"It won't take long," Clint said. "Five minutes."

Kenny turned around and looked at his two tables, then back at Clint.

"You can come into the kitchen with me."

"Okay," Clint said, "thanks."

Kenny led Clint into the busy kitchen. Waiters were moving back and forth, while two more men worked over two hot stoves. Clint wondered what the kitchen in a large restaurant must be like.

"What can I do for you?" Kenny asked.

He and Clint both had to move aside for another waiter carrying a heavily laden tray to walk by.

"You waited on Bat Masterson the morning he was arrested, right?"

"Yes, sir," Kenny said.

"How do you remember?"

"Everyone remembers that morning, sir," Kenny said. "There was a lot of excitement that morning."

"Did you see anyone who might have been paying special attention to Masterson?" Clint asked.

"How do you mean, sir?" Kenny asked. "I know I was paying special attention to him."

"Well, yeah, he was your customer," Clint said. "I mean maybe somebody from the lobby watching him?"

Kenny thought a moment, then said, "No, sir. Of course, it was our breakfast rush at the time. I really didn't have time to look out into the lobby."

"I see," Clint said. "Well, if you remember anything, would you please find me and let me know?" He gave the man a dollar.

"I sure will, sir. Thank you."

Clint left the restaurant and walked to the front desk. The clerk on duty was the same one who had signed him in when he arrived.

"Excuse me, what's your name?" he asked

"Gilbert, sir."

"Gilbert, who was working the desk the morning Bat Masterson was arrested?"

"I was, sir."

"Good. I need to ask you a few questions."

"Of course, sir."

"Did you see Mr. Masterson that morning."

"Yes, sir."

"When?"

"When he came in to have breakfast," Gilbert said. "I saw him go into the restaurant, and then saw him come out and go upstairs."

"Did you hear a shot?"

"No, sir."

"When was the first time you realized something was wrong?" Clint asked.

"Mr. Masterson came down and asked me to send someone for the Sheriff."

"How soon after he went up did he come down?"

"Oh, it was only minutes."

"And what did he do while you sent for the Sheriff?"

"He waited here in the lobby, sir."

"And he didn't go up again without the Sheriff?"

"No, sir."

"Did you see anyone go upstairs right before Mr. Masterson went up?"

"Not that I recall, sir."

"How about anybody who came down right after he went up? Or just before he came down?"

"No, sir. I don't recall anyone."

"Is there another stairway down from upstairs?"

"No, sir. This is the only way up."

"What room was Mr. Masterson in?"

"Room Twelve, sir."

"Is there anyone in that room now?"

"No, sir. We haven't even moved Mr. Masterson's belongings out."

"Good," Clint said. "I'd like to take a look inside. Can you give me a key?"

"Of course, sir."

The clerk turned, plucked a key from a slot, and then handed it to Clint.

"Are you trying to prove he didn't do it, sir?"

"That's what I'm doing, yes."

"Well," Gilbert said, "I wish you luck, sir."

Sensing that the young man was completely sincere Clint said, "Thank you."

THIRTY-NINE

Clint walked to room twelve and used the key to get inside. Just as the clerk had said, Bat's belongings were still there. A set of saddlebags, a rifle, and a carpetbag with clean shirts in it. Clint grabbed one of the shirts, hung it on the doorknob so he wouldn't forget it.

He walked around the room, checked the window. It was a sheer two story drop to the ground. Nobody got in that way. He walked to the door, checked to see if anyone had forced it. The lock was intact, wasn't new so it hadn't been replaced recently. No jimmy marks around it. So there was only one way Cable could have gotten into the room.

With a key.

He took the fresh shirt off the doorknob and left the room.

Downstairs he went back to the front desk.

"If I find out you gave Cable Lockheart a key to Bat's room—" he said to the kid at the desk.

"Huh? What? No, no, sir. I never give anybody keys

to the guest's rooms. Mister, some day I wanna be the manager of a hotel. I start givin' out keys I'll never get that job."

Clint looked into the young man's eyes and believed what he was saying.

"Okay, who else works the desk?" he asked.

"Got three other clerks," the man said.

"Write down their names and where I can find them."

The kid got a piece of paper, wrote down the three names.

"Save me some time, son," Clint said. "Which one of these would most likely give somebody a key for money."

"For money? Delbert."

Clint looked at the names. Delbert Conroy.

"Why did you say it like that. 'For money'? Would there be another reason?"

"I don't know if I should say," the clerk replied.

"I think you should," Clint said, staring him straight in the eye.

"Okay," Gilbert said, "Willis has a crush on Angie, Cable's girl."

Gilbert didn't know that Cable and Angie were related.

"So?"

"If Cable had promised to get them together, Willis might've gave him a key."

Clint looked at the list again. Willis Green.

"Okay, Gilbert, thanks."

"You won't tell them I talked to you?" Gilbert asked, nervously.

"Don't worry, Gilbert," Clint said. "This is just between you and me."

"Thank you, sir."

"Of course, if I find out you're lying to me . . ."

"I swear, Mr. Adams, I ain't lyin'," Gilbert said.

"Okay, Gilbert," Clint said. "Thanks for the help,"

He left the hotel, headed for the rooming house Angie had told him she lived in.

Before he could reach the rooming house, though, he ran into Tom Nolan.

"Tom I can't talk—"

"Come on, Clint," the man said. "Ya gotta gimme somethin' to do. I wanna help!"

"Okay," Clint said, thinking fast, "I tell you what you can do. The hat shop girl, Mandy? Keep your ear to the ground. The Sheriff still has nothing on who killed her."

"Well, yeah, okay, I can do that," Nolan said. "Shame for a pretty girl to die like that. I mean, strangled with her own scarf? Terrible."

"Yes, I know, Tom," Clint said. "Look, I have to go. Let me know if you hear anything."

"Sure thing."

FORTY

He knocked on the door, told the landlady who he wanted to see.

"No men in my rooms," she said firmly.

"I'll wait out here," he promised.

She went inside. In a few minutes Angie came out.

"Oh," she said.

"Were you expecting Mason?"

"I didn't know."

"You know a man named Green, Willis Green?"

"Willis? Well, sure."

"How?"

"We grew up together."

"So he knows you and Cable were cousins?"

"Well, sure."

Obviously, Green hadn't told Gilbert that part.

"If you grew up around here why doesn't the whole town know that you're cousins with Cable and Mason?"

"We grew up outside of town," she said. "Didn't come in much. When I got old enough I come in and got a job, didn't admit who I was. I used a different last name. Harlan."

"So your real last name is Lockheart?"

"Yeah."

"Green has a crush on you?"

"Sure, ever since we was kids. He used to peek at us when—" She stopped short.

"Peek at you and who? Cable? Mason?"

"Cable," she said. "We was kids, and curious. We used to . . . fool around a bit."

"Naked?"

She nodded.

"Green saw you?"

"When I was thirteen."

"And he's wanted you ever since."

"I guess."

"So if Cable wanted the key to Bat's room, and offered you up in return, Green would have given it to him?"

"I guess, only I wasn't Cable's to give."

"Yeah, well, Willis Green wouldn't have to know that."

"I suppose not."

Clint took a moment to think.

"What's wrong?"

"What if Willis Green did know that?" he asked. "What if he knew Cable would never help him with you?"

"I don't understand—"

"Did Willis hate Cable?"

"Why?"

"Because he's been with you and Willis hasn't," Clint said. "Maybe because he knew Cable would never help him?"

"So you think Willis killed Cable? He ain't a killer, Clint. He's a coward."

"What if he let somebody else do it for him?"

"Like who?"

"I guess maybe that's a question I'm going to have to ask him," Clint said. He showed Angie the piece of paper Gilbert had written on. "Is this where I can find him?"

She looked at the paper. Her eyes widened for a moment, and then she said, "I guess."

"What's wrong?"

"Nothin'," she said, turning away.

"Angie."

"It's nothin', I tell you," she said. "It ain't got nothin' to do with nothin'."

"Why don't you let me be the judge of that?" he asked.

She hesitated, hugging her upper arms like she was cold.

"The other name on that list."

"Which one?"

"John Tucker."

That was the third name.

"What about him?"

"He also grew up with us."

"And?"

She looked at him, then looked away.

"When I was fourteen?"

"Yeah?"

She turned her back, like she couldn't look at him when she said, "He raped me."

FORTY-ONE

"I never told Cable or Mason," she said. "They woulda killed him."

"So you let him get away with it?"

She shrugged.

"Maybe it wasn't rape."

"Maybe?"

"I had just been in the barn with Cable," she said. "We went . . . further than we ever had before."

"Further?"

"Okay," she said "we did it. He left, and I was getting' dressed. Johnny came in. I was still mostly naked. He said he'd watched, and if I didn't do it with him, he'd tell."

"So you did it?"

"I didn't want to. He started to force me, so I figured just let him do it and leave. He was . . . bigger than Cable . . . and he hurt me, but when he was finished he left. I cried, got dressed and never told."

"And what happened?

"Nothin'," she said. "I stopped doin' stuff with Cable. I guess he thought it as because we went too far."

"And what about Tucker?"

"He was still around, but he acted like nothin' ever happened."

"And Green?"

"He just . . . followed me around like a puppy."

"So Green could have killed Cable, or given someone the chance to do it. Or John Tucker could have killed him."

"But why?"

"Maybe Cable found out what he did."

"After all these years? Cable wouldn't care."

"Maybe he would've. What would Mason do if you told him now?"

"He'd kill John."

"Where is Mason now? Where's he staying?"

"Out at the old house."

"Okay," he said. "You stay here."

"What are you gonna do?"

"I'm going to go and see all these men," he said, "and Mason, but first I have to deliver a shirt."

FORTY-TWO

Clint rushed to the courthouse, found that court was not in session yet. There were spectators seated in the room, but the bench was empty.

Lee Martin was sitting at a table near the front of the courtroom. Clint walked up, tapped him on the shoulder.

"Where's Bat?"

"In there, with the Sheriff." He was pointing to a door.

Clint walked over and knocked. Sheriff Deming opened it.

"What do you want, Adams? We're about to go into court."

"Bat deserves to look decent," Clint said. "I brought him a fresh shirt."

"Well, give it to me and I'll let him have it."

"And let you take the credit?"

Deming looked exasperated.

"All right. Come in."

Clint entered.

"Your gun?"

He handed it over.

"Two minutes," Deming said, and stepped out.

Bat was sitting at a long table, waiting.

"Hey," he said.

Clint tossed him the shirt.

"Thanks." He stood up, took off his jacket and the grimy shirt.

"Wouldn't happen to have a bath on you, would you?"

"Sorry."

Bat slipped into the fresh shirt.

"That feels good," he said, buttoning it. "Thanks."

"I've got a few names to check today, Bat," Clint said. "I think this whole thing was personal, maybe even extends from childhood."

"Sounds promising."

"Just stall," Clint said. "Stall as long as you can."

"Maybe," Bat said, "I can get the Judge into a poker game."

"Do whatever you have to do," Clint said. "I think I'm close."

"I hope so, Clint."

"Don't worry, Bat," Clint said. "Whatever happens, I'll get you out."

The two friends shook hands, and Clint left.

He told Lee Martin everything he had told Bat, and gave him the same "Stall as long as you can" message.

He left the courthouse and walked to the livery stable. His first intention had been to talk to all the desk clerks, but now he decided to go and see Mason Locke first.

Maybe having him along when he talked to those men would be helpful.

That is, if Mason Locke felt like being helpful.

Clint followed Angie's directions, found the old house where she had grown up. There was a leanto nearby, with a horse in it. Apparently, Mason Locke was staying there alone. Red Cassiday was probably back in town.

Clint dismounted, waited to see if he had been noticed.

"Locke?" he called. "Mason Locke?"

"I see you," Locke said.

"I just want to talk."

"So talk."

"Angie told me how to get here," Clint said. "It's about Cable."

After a moment the front door opened and Locke stepped out. He was wearing his gun, but his hands were on his belt.

"So talk."

"I think I know who killed Cable."

"Who?"

"One of two men," Clint said. "We just have to find out which one."

"And set Masterson free?"

"That's right, because he didn't do it."

"Who?"

"Willis Green or John Tucker."

Locke frowned.

"Do I know them?"

"They're both hotel clerks at my hotel," Clint said, "but Angie knew them when she was growing up."

Clint wondered if Mason Locke knew that Angie and Cable used to play around as kids. If not, how would he react? Could he explain about Green and Tucker without telling him that?

He tried.

"They had access to keys," Clint said, after he explained who they were.

"I remember Green," he said. "He's a milk toast."

"What does it take to sneak up on a man and shoot him?" Clint asked.

"And Tucker?"

"You don't remember him?"

"No," Locke said, shaking his head slowly. "He was friends with Angie?"

"Actually," Clint said, "he was also . . . sweet on her, only he was a little more aggressive than Green."

"Green or Tucker," Locke said.

"If we work together—"

"Or split up," Locke said. "We'd get finished faster that way."

"Okay," Clint said, "So we're working together?"

"Just until we catch my brother's killer," Locke said, "whoever he turns out to be."

"Okay, who do you want?"

"I'll take Green," Locke said. "He'll remember me."

"Okay, I'll take John Tucker."

"If it turns out to be Tucker," Locke said. "Bring him here."

"No," Clint said, "we take the guilty one to court."

"One of us has to let the other one know what's goin' on," Locke said. "We bring him here, and then we bring him to court."

"It'll take too long that way," Clint said. "Let's meet somewhere in town."

"Okay," Locke said, "the Big Pine Saloon."

"Agreed."

"Where do I find Green?"

FORTY-THREE

John Tucker rented a room from a widow who owned a house on the edge of town. When Clint knocked he expected the door to be answered by an elderly woman. Instead, the widow turned out to be a beautiful brunette in her mid-forties.

"Yes?"

"I'm looking for John Tucker," he said.

"Johnny? What for?"

"I have some questions for him," he said. "Does he live here?"

"He does," she said, looking Clint up and down. "He pays rent."

"Is he here now?"

"He is."

"Is he . . . busy?"

He hadn't interrupted anything. Her hair and clothes were too neat for that.

"Yes. I'll get him. Would you like to wait inside?"

"Thank you."

She led him to the living room, then said, "I'll get him."

He remained standing while he waited. She returned with a handsome young man Angie's age. He was dressed in a clean shirt and black trousers that probably had a matching jacket somewhere. Dressing for work. No gun.

"Who are you?" he asked. "Whataya want?"

Clint looked at the woman.

"It's my house," she said, crossing her arms.

"What's your name?"

"Mrs. Ford."

"Well, Mrs. Ford, you might hear something you don't want to hear."

"I'll take my chances," she said.

"Hey, what the hell is goin' on?" Tucker demanded.

"This is about Cable Lockheart," Clint said to him, "and his cousin, Angie. You remember Angie, don't you? You raped her when she was fourteen?"

"W-what the hell—" Tucker said. He looked at Mrs. Ford, then back to Clint. "T-that wasn't rape. She wanted it."

Clint and Mrs. Ford stared at him.

"She was doin' it with her own cousin!" Tucker said. "Why not me?"

"I'm not worried about that, Tucker," Clint said. "You work at the hotel where Cable was killed."

"So?" Then his eyes widened. "You think I did that?"

"Or you gave somebody a key to do it."

"L-look," Thomas said, "I'm the one who gave Cable a key to Masterson's room, b-but I didn't kill him."

"Then who did?"

"I don't know. I swear!"

"No one else went up after Cable?"

"Masterson."

"So you were on duty that night?"

"No, Gilbert worked the night shift."

"What time did the night shift end?"

"Six a.m."

So someone else came on at six. Gilbert hadn't told him that.

"Tucker, who came on duty at six?"

Clint went to the Big Pine Saloon, found Mason Locke waiting for him . . . alone, except for a beer.

"Beer," Clint told the bartender.

"So Tucker didn't do it?" Locke asked.

"No," Clint said, "I'm sure of it. Green?"

Locke shook his head.

"He groveled at my feet, begged me not to kill him. I believe he didn't kill Cable."

"There's a third man," Clint said. "Do you know Delbert Conroy?"

"Conroy? He's a clerk at the hotel, too?"

"Yes, why?"

"Why didn't you tell me that before?" Locke demanded.

"Why?" Clint asked again.

"Conroy hates my family," Locke said. "Always has."

"Don't tell me he's always been sweet on Angie, too," Clint said.

"No," Locke said, "nobody in my family would have anything to do with the Conroy family."

"You know what I'm wondering?" Clint asked.

"What?"

"How did all three of these men, who have history with your family, end up working at that hotel?"

"Coincidence," Locke said. "It's not that big a town."

"They just happen to work in the hotel where Cable was killed?" Clint asked. "I don't like that kind of coincidence."

"What if Cable just happened to get killed in the hotel where those three men worked?" Locke said.

"Is there a difference?"

Locke shrugged.

"Maybe not."

FORTY-FOUR

"What makes you think he'll be here?" Clint asked Locke.

"He wasn't at the hotel," Locke said. "This is the house his family has always lived in."

"It's not far from yours."

"I know."

"So your families were neighbors?"

"Yes."

"And learned to hate each other?"

"Yes."

"So seeing Cable go up to Masterson's room, Conroy saw his chance to kill him. He used his key, got the drop on Cable, disarmed him and killed him with his own gun."

"That sounds logical. But how did Cable get into Bat's room?"

"Tucker," Clint said. "He told me he gave Cable the key."

They were both mounted, having ridden their horses to the Conroy house.

"Let's take him," Locke said.

"Without killing him," Clint said. "I need him to get Bat free."

Locke hesitated, then nodded.

They dismounted.

Judge Rupert Reilly slammed his gavel down savagely, demanding silence in the court room. He glared at the defense table, where Lee Martin sat next to Bat Masterson.

"Mr. Martin," he said, "I'm growin' very tired of these delayin' tactics of yours."

"Sorry, your honor," Martin said. "I'm just—"

"Would you mind tellin' me just what you're hoping to achieve?"

Well, what Martin was hoping to achieve was to give Clint Adams enough time to march the real killer right into court. And just when he thought that he and Bat had run out of time, the back doors slammed open and three men came barging in.

The spectators got excited and Reilly had to slam his gavel down again, and shout, "Order in my court!"

Clint and Mason Locke stopped in the aisle, with a third man between them.

"Mr. Adams?" Reilly said. "Would you mind tellin' me why you're interruptin' my court?"

"Well, your honor," Clint said, "Mr. Locke and I have something important to tell the court."

"Locke?" Reilly asked.

"Mason Locke," Locke said.

"The gunman?" the Judge asked.

"The brother of the victim, your honor," Mason Locke said.

That brought noise from the gallery again, and Reilly used his gavel again.

"Anymore of that and I'll clear this court room!" he shouted.

Everyone fell silent.

"Mr. Adams, Mr. Locke, what is so important, and who is this third young man? Another gunfighter?"

"Not at all, your honor," Clint said. "This is Delbert Conroy, a citizen of Sweetwater. He is also a clerk at the Cherry Blossom Hotel, where Cable Lockheart was killed."

"So far, none of this is very enlightenin'," Reilly said. "You'll have to do better."

"We intend to, your honor," Clint said. "Delbert Conroy is also the man who actually killed Cable Lockheart."

Reilly grabbed his gavel, in anticipation of needing it, but everyone in the room had been struck dumb.

"Is this true?" Judge Reilly asked Conroy.

Conroy looked at the Judge, then said, "Yes, sir."

"Are you being coerced into this confession, young man?" Reilly asked.

"Huh?"

"Are you saying this because you fear these two men?" Reilly asked.

"I ain't afraid of nobody," Conroy said, belligerently.

"Why did you kill Cable Lockheart?"

Conroy looked at the Judge as if he was crazy.

"Because he was a Lockheart," he said, finally. "Conroys and Lockhearts been killin' each other fer years."

"But why now? You've had plenty of time to kill him in the past."

"He come into the hotel where I work," Conroy said. "He didn't even see me. Somebody else gave him a key to Bat Masterson's room. So I followed him up with my gun."

"You shot him with your gun?" the Judge asked, trying to trip up his confession.

"No, sir. I got the drop on him, took his gun and shot him with that."

"Then what?"

"Then I lit out."

"And left Mr. Masterson to take the blame?"

"That's right."

"So why are you here now?"

"These fellers found me, they told me they knew I killed Cable. And this one, here—" he indicated Mason Locke, "—he's a Lockheart. So I couldn't lie to him. I killed his brother."

"Did he threaten to kill you?"

"No, sir," Conroy said, "he tol' me I had to come here to court and tell you what I done."

Judge Reilly looked over at the defense table, scowled at Masterson, then looked at Sheriff Deming.

"Sheriff," he said, "release Mr. Masterson and out this man under arrest."

"Yes, sir."

"Mr. Masterson," Reilly said, "in light of this confession you are free to go—but don't let me catch you in my court again."

"Don't worry, Judge," Bat said. "I'll be out of this town, and this country, by tomorrow."

"That sounds like a very good idea," Reilly said. he slammed his gavel down one last time.

"This court is adjourned!"

FORTY-FIVE

Clint woke the next morning with the now familiar naked form of Angie next to him.

"Are you really leaving today?" she asked.

"Yes, I am. This morning."

"There's nothing I can do to change your mind?" she asked, sliding one leg over him.

"Well," he said, "you can convince me to leave later . . ."

She smiled, reached between them, found his already hard cock with her hand and guided it into her. She gasped as he slid into her fully, and then she began to ride him up and down, her hands on the bed post, her tits in his face.

It was very distracting.

He bit her nipples while she rode him, grinding herself down on him. He grabbed her ass in both hands and held it, still biting and sucking as she rubbed her breasts in his face until, finally, he exploded inside of her . . .

* * *

They got dressed together, and, while she wasn't looking, he slid his Colt New Line into his belt at the small of his back.

"Can we have breakfast?" she asked.

"No," he replied. "I've got to meet Bat out front. We're leaving town together."

"Well," she said, "I'll come down to the street with you and see you off."

"That'd be great," he said.

He let her leave ahead of him, carried his saddlebags and rifle out into the hall.

Outside Red Cassiday said to Mason Locke, "You sure you wanna do it this way, Mace?"

"This is the only way I wanna do it, Red," Locke said. "Don't worry about it."

In front of the hotel they saw Bat Masterson waiting with both his horse and Clint's.

"What about Masterson?" Red asked.

"We'll take care of him," Locke said, "after."

While they watched Clint came out of the hotel with Angie.

"'Mornin' Bat," Clint said.

"Clint. Ready to go?"

"Ready as I'll ever be?"

"Did you say a proper goodbye?"

"Oh yeah," Clint said, "we had a real nice goodbye."

"Adams!"

Clint and Bat both looked in the direction of the voice. Mason Locke stepped down into the street.

"Locke," Clint said. "Come to say goodbye?"

"You didn't really think you were gonna get out of town without facin' me, did you?" Locke asked.

"Well," Clint said, "I kind of thought since we proved together who killed your brother, we'd pretty much skip this part."

"Sorry," Locke said, "it don't work that way. I can't let you leave."

Clint sighed.

"I didn't think so."

Clint handed Bat his saddlebags and rifle.

"Keep an eye on Cassiday," he said. "I don't think he'll try anything, but just in case."

"I gotcha."

Clint turned to Angie.

"You better stand aside, Angie."

"Clint—" she said, but he cut her off.

"Hey," he said, "I know, family comes first."

She frowned at him, not understanding for a moment, and then when she did she threw a look toward Mason Locke.

It was too late, though, Locke was completely focused on Clint.

When Clint stepped down into the street she saw the gun in the back of his belt, and knew.

"What do you say, Mason?" Clint asked. "Think about it, and forget it. This doesn't have to happen."

"This always has to happen with men like you and me, Adams," Locke said. "You knew that as soon as I came to town, just like I did."

"Then I'm sorry," Clint said.

"Why?" Locke asked. "Don't tell me you expected to die in bed of old age?"

"Well, no," Clint said, "I don't expect that, and I don't expect to die today, either."

"Sorry to disappoint you," Mason Locke said, and went for his gun.

He was fast.

Almost too fast, since Clint had to reach behind him for the New Line, and not to the unloaded Colt in his holster.

He brought the New Line around, saw the surprised look on Locke's face as he pulled the trigger. It was a small caliber gun, but the bullet was well laced. It hit Locke right in the heart. He staggered, coughed, gun in hand. He tried to lift it, so Clint had to fire a second time. This one hit Locke in the lungs. When he coughed again blood flowed from his mouth.

He fell face down in the street . . .

FORTY-SIX

Red Cassiday stepped into the street as Locke fell to the ground, his hand on his gun.

"Don't even think about it!" Bat Masterson warned him.

Red looked at Bat, who had not drawn his gun, then looked at his fallen friend.

"He was my friend," Red said.

"And Clint is mine," Bat said. "And you and me, Red, we can walk away.

Red thought about it but in the end, with a tear in his eyes, he said, to Bat, "I can't."

"Don't—" Bat said, but Red went for it.

Bat drew and fired once . . .

With Mason Locke and Red Cassiday both lying in the street, dead, Clint turned and faced Angie.

"You killed him!" she said.

Bat came up alongside Clint.

"What's with the little gun?" he asked.

Clint tucked the new Line into his belt, then drew the Colt and snapped it open, showing Bat the empty cylinder. One by one he replaced the live loads, and holstered it.

"She emptied it during our goodbye," he said. "Thought she could distract me with her body while she unloaded it."

"But . . . why? I thought Mason Locke wanted to take you fair and square?"

"It just had to look fair," Clint said. "Right, Angie?"

"He asked me to do it," she said. "He's the last of my family, and you . . . you were goon' to leave me!"

"Still am," he said. He turned, saw Sheriff Deming coming towards them at a fast pace. "Soon as we explain everything to the Sheriff."

"Are you . . . are you gonna tell him about me?" she asked.

"I don't know, Angie," Clint said. "Should I? Maybe you better get moving, just in case."

A tear streaked down her face, but he didn't feel sorry for her. She'd made her choice.

He turned, watched the Sheriff approach them, at the same time noticing Tom Nolan across the street, watching the proceedings.

"Adams, what the hell?" Deming demanded.

"Not my choice, Sheriff," Clint said. "Locke and Cassiday pushed it."

"He's right, Sheriff," Bat said.

"Who shot who?" Deming demanded.

"I shot Locke, Bat killed Cassiday."

"Damn it," Deming said, "you couldn't get out of town without doin' it, could you. I should haul you both in."

"I don't think you'll want to do that when I tell you what just hit me."

"What are you talkin' about?"

"Tom Nolan, over there."

Deming turned, looked at Nolan, then turned back.

"What about him?"

"You might ask him how he knew that Mandy Stuart was strangled with her own scarf."

"What? Did you tell him that?"

"I didn't tell him a thing," Clint said. "He told me."

Deming thought about it, then said, "Mount up and get out of town.

Watch for

UNBOUND BY LAW

352nd novel in the exciting GUNSMITH series
from Jove

Coming in April!